MELTDOWN

by

C.A.S Novel

**Grosvenor House
Publishing Limited**

All rights reserved
Copyright © C.A.S Novel, 2012

C.A.S Novel is hereby identified as author of this
work in accordance with Section 77 of the Copyright, Designs
and Patents Act 1988

The book cover picture is copyright to Inmagine Corp LLC

This book is published by
Grosvenor House Publishing Ltd
28-30 High Street, Guildford, Surrey, GU1 3EL.
www.grosvenorhousepublishing.co.uk

This book is sold subject to the conditions that it shall not, by way of
trade or otherwise, be lent, resold, hired out or otherwise circulated
without the author's or publisher's prior consent in any form of binding or
cover other than that in which it is published and
without a similar condition including this condition being imposed
on the subsequent purchaser.

A CIP record for this book
is available from the British Library

ISBN 978-1-78148-562-0

Notes about the Author

Derbyshire-born author Christopher Albert Summerfield (C.A.S.) likes to create work that appeals to him, something gritty and dark, though there's always hope in his stories. He loves the authors Susan Hill, Ian Rankin and Irvine Welsh.

Dedications

*To family past and present; there
is a place in my heart for you all.
To my editor, Sarah; thanks for your hard work.
To the film director and writer
Geno McGahee; thanks for your support.
To my close friends; you know who you are.
And to all who believe in me; bless you all,
and may all your dreams come true.*

1

MELTDOWN

Day 1

LONDON KING'S CROSS

5.52 p.m.

There were suited people, casually dressed people, all either heading into or out of King's Cross tube station, most, though, with their heads down, just wanting to reach their destinations, none bothered about who was around them. People, just viewed as obstacles they just had to get around, just eager to get to where they wished, away from the madness and to their own sanctuaries, their safe havens.

And to make their surroundings less visible to the mind's eye, less conscious of the misery, they all used modern distractions, some being in the form of iPods, others MP3 players, listening to something upbeat, something to lift them, give them a much-needed boost, most, though, with mobiles, either attached to their ears or in their hands, texting away.

Yet, with all these distractions they could all still sense the gloom which seemed heavy in the air, uncertainty upon the many faces. Evident of what was worrying the masses everywhere; closing down sales here and there, job losses going through the roof, everybody affected, even stories going around about the alarming rise in suicides.

And the word everybody dreaded being spoken everywhere: Recession! Recession! Recession!

So much uncertainty, so much doubt, so much suffering ahead for all, even bound to be more suicides. Yes, the root of all evil surely spreading its bad karma; the devil disguised as banknotes.

Newspaper headlines quoting: *Destined to be the worst recession since the 1930s.*

Everybody being warned to brace themselves for the worst. Yes, worse to come. A hell of a lot worse to come. So sanctuary in oneself was needed, an escape justifiable.

5.54 p.m.

Then suddenly, there was an almighty roar caused by an explosion, which shook the whole capital, shattering windows and shaking buildings, people bumping into each other, being thrown to the ground, left dazed and wondering for a while; children crying, dogs barking, alarms blaring, traffic at a standstill, all wondering where it had happened, how it had happened.

And the explosion seemed to have happened very close by, somewhere in Central London, as there was smoke billowing out from that direction – thick dark-green smoke, thick green smoke that seemed to be over-running the dark-blue sky, choking the city.

Everybody around King's Cross paralysed with shock, shocked out of their own little worlds, all looking around at each other for answers, everyone becoming visible, some having to get back to their feet where they had fallen. Sirens deafening as the emergency services screamed in the direction of Central London, people muttering away, assumptions being exchanged. All then staring in disbelief at the green smog that seemed to be rising from the drains, similar to the thick green smoke from the explosion, but diluted; all expecting something, but not sure what – the recession seeming to be the least important thing to think about.

And what followed within such a short time was...

There was a scream, then a man soaked in blood appeared near the tube station. He seemed to have appeared from nowhere, and was screaming something about people killing people, and telling people to run for their lives. Saliva seemed to be pouring out of his mouth, his eyes rolling, insanity not far away. Then he just collapsed to his knees and choked, and continued to choke and vomit, with traces of blood. And all people could do was stare, just stare, shocked by what they were seeing, what they were hearing, though not sure what to do or what to expect; all looking at each other, wanting some victim to take charge, all feeling alienated with the thought of working together, though all trying their best to cover their mouths, expecting the green smog to choke them, so they would end up like the man before them.

Then suddenly, the street lights began to fade, plunging shops and office blocks into darkness, though the alarms continued blaring. People got back in their cars, wanting to get the hell out of there, but were stopped by the other cars, all gridlocked, people using their horns and shouting, desperation kicking in, the sound of tyres squealing as drivers became frantic, people shuddering as cars collided, all desperate to escape.

Then the panic really started, as suddenly, there appeared a large crowd of people, all looking agitated, screaming and roaring, wild and possessed. They suddenly charged at a group of people just a stone's throw away from King's Cross; the group of about half a dozen or more people had appeared from a shop, taken shelter in there and, on impact, attacked them, showing no mercy, just hell-bent on murder.

The crowd at King's Cross had just watched in horror, as if they were watching a horror movie, unable to interact, unable to shape events, but expecting the worst. Then they heard a loud scream and turned to see the man who had been choking in front of them strangling a woman, a woman who had gone to his aid, strangling her with sheer brutal hatred.

The people standing around outside King's Cross then came back to life, one of them shouting something about a chemical attack, saying it was sending people mad; all not wanting to be where they were, most following their basic instinct and running for their lives, drivers taking desperate measures to get out of there, mounting kerbs and hitting pedestrians, tossing them over the car bonnet as if they were trash; none wanting to help the woman as her life was choked away.

And like a sweeping tide, within minutes if not seconds the hysteria seemed to have spread across the city, nobody knowing what was happening, just listening to assumptions and running for their lives. People were trying to text, trying to call, but lines were busy or there was too much interference; using mobile cameras to film what they were witnessing, as if they were amateur film directors, the next Romero.

Then within the blink of an eye things got worse, as there was another explosion and more billowing green smoke seemed to cause all forms of communication to crash, everything from mobiles to landlines. No Internet, nothing.

People found themselves alone, trying desperately to make their mobiles work, to make that call to someone or to summon help, and as it became evident they couldn't, they suddenly found themselves terrified. The only thing left to do was fight for survival against people that had gone mad, people they had probably passed in the street at sometime in their lives, but were there and then trying to escape them, as they were just killing others in what was a mindless slaughter; people being reduced to hysteria and murder, human carnage on a scale nobody had ever witnessed. Just mindless slaughter, no sense or clarity in why.

The whole city besieged by terror. The roads gridlocked with cars trying to leave and cars trying to enter London, all considering it to be the right decision. The skies also besieged by helicopters, VIPs and those that could afford to pay being flown out of the city; the privileged few being looked after.

And as time passed and the city became darker, the slaughter intensified and there were no signs of law and order. No signs at all. Looters then striking, hitting the shops that hadn't used their steel shutters, smashing windows, robbing shops of their contents, and those that were brave enough to try to stop them, a handful of security guards, either pushed through the broken windows or beaten to death; no mercy for nobody.

People continuing to run for their lives, seeking refuge, seeking sanctuary from what they were witnessing, being exposed to.

And King's Cross, just like everywhere else, was no refuge as the many that had stood about had sensed the danger and fled. Yet there were some people standing around wondering what to do next. They had been on the move just like the masses, but having exhausted all possibilities they now stood around dazed, confused and tired.

And one of those people who was standing there, not sure what to do, was Mary Sanders.

Mary stood on the corner of York Way, trying to digest what was happening while holding her son close to her breasts, trying to shield him from the butchery that was going on around them.

The reason for her being there?

She had been spurred on by where she wanted to be, where she believed it would be safe, but was becoming more desperate about how she was going to get there.

And her purpose for moving was because home was no longer safe, had become far too dangerous. They may have lost their lives like so many other people they knew if they had remained, but then again it wasn't safe anywhere, and the only other place she could think of was where her husband Jamie worked.

Jamie worked near Euston Square, and she would reach him if she were to use the Underground. That had been her plan on abandoning the car; the only option left. But to do so she would have to cross the road, becoming visible to a riotous mob that were trashing shops, restaurants and bars, and mercilessly attacking anyone and everyone, regardless of age and sex.

And during her desperate flight to where she found herself there and then, not once had she seen any sign of the law.

It seemed to her as if it had dissolved under the spell of green smog and it was now a 'free for all'. Looters, murderers and rapists, they were everywhere, visible at every turn. It seemed to her that the city had been overrun with evil and there seemed no refuge from what she was witnessing.

Suddenly, a bus came hurtling along the road, headlights cutting through the smog and darkness, horn screaming; it came like a demon racing from hell, weaving in and out of stationary cars, cars that had been abandoned. Then the screeching of brakes, then seconds later, impact!

Everyone within the vicinity shuddered, not daring to look.

The bus had crashed into the back of a stationary car, shunting it into another stationary one. As for the bus driver, his head had exploded against the windscreen, thick red blood running down the shattered glass, and the sound of the horn screaming as the deceased driver lay upon it.

The riotous mob suddenly paused, stared at the bus that was screaming at them and charged at it. The passengers on the bus looked terrified, clinging onto their belongings and loved ones, watching helplessly as the mob forced the doors open.

And as the mob boarded, the passengers began screaming, unsure what to do but expecting the worst. Continuing to hold onto their loved ones and belongings, crouching and hoping they would be shown mercy, the mob showed no mercy as they entered the bus, biting, gauging, stabbing and squeezing the life out of men, women and children, just hell-bent on slaughter, no one to be left alive.

Then the fire exit burst open and a suited man jumped out. His face was pale, gripped with terror; he was clinging on to a case containing his life's possessions, but he was met by a speeding car, his bones shattering upon impact, his lifeless body being tossed into the air like a rag doll.

As for the car which had hit him, it screeched and swerved until finally crashing into the railings and exploding, cremating all the passengers apart from one – a woman who had managed to get out of the car but was engulfed in flames. Screaming and fumbling around, she finally collapsed to her knees, gargling and withering away.

As for Mary, she had just continued to watch, like so many others. Just watching, too petrified to move. Just waiting to possibly be the next victim, although hoping for a miracle in the form of the law arriving.

She then became aware of the beating of a helicopter overhead. Not a passenger one like the ones that were about earlier; this one was smaller and hovered, with a beam of light coming from it, scanning the carnage, a camera filming what was happening.

Just filming.

Just fucking filming.

Filming a real-life horror show.

A snuff film.

Then two suited women came rushing past her looking extremely stressed and nearly knocked her over.

She glared at them, but like everyone else they were just running, unfazed by her, just trying to escape the crazed mobs that were everywhere.

Mary then glanced behind her to see half a dozen people running towards them, screaming wildly, snot and saliva flying from their faces, eyes rolling.

Just like the rest of the mobs, they looked crazed and out of control, like those that were attacking the passengers on the bus. Those that were on her street, on every street she had been on. And these were heading in her direction, just like those on her street had been: destination Mary.

Mary and her son's turn, unless she moved, and she had witnessed first-hand what they would do to them if they reached them; the way they had slaughtered her neighbours, slaughtered everybody and anybody they had come into contact with.

Mary then glanced in the direction of the suited women, wondering where they were heading, and saw the tallest leading the other into King's Cross tube station, no one following them.

The tube station she was destined for, had longed to reach.

She then wondered, hoped, that perhaps the tube station was still operational; then within the next fifteen minutes she could be in Euston Square. Ten minutes later, in her husband's arms.

The noise all around was petrifying, gripping the muscles, not letting them dare move, the reason they had been stationary for the past five minutes. The urgency to move, though, was so great, and to move fast.

So without a second thought she headed for the station, trying to block out the screams and cries for help while clinging tightly on to her son's hand, not daring to look around, dreading a hand grasping her or even worse grasping her son. Blind panic leading her, guiding her, her fear gripping her, driving her on.

Moments later, she reached the tube station and allowed herself to sigh. Her breathing was heavy and laboured, but without glancing around she hurried down the stairs, son at her side, the sound of their shoes pounding, echoing in her ears. The sound was alarming, frightening herself with her own urgency to reach her destination, plunging deeper into darkness, not sure what to expect, wondering if she was making the right decision, praying and hoping the journey would be worth it.

Fifteen minutes, Euston.

Ten minutes later, in her husband's arms.

Suddenly, she paused as she reached Level 1. The whole area deserted, she couldn't hear any voices; perhaps they were on their own. She then noticed that the signs indicating when trains would arrive and where they were destined weren't working. Then again, neither were the lights.

Just maybe the trains were running, but deep down she knew the truth, she just didn't want to believe it. She would have to see it to believe it.

Rather than continuing to head for the platform she paused for a moment, trying to calm herself down so she could think clearly. Give herself time to question her sanity, as it was destined to get darker the deeper underground they went.

And what if there were some of those crazed people down there?

The thought was too terrifying to spend too much time considering.

Then, as her eyes began to adapt to the darkness, she began noticing personal items scattered here and there, sure signs of panic and hysteria. The fare gates had also been forced open, confirming the hysteria, and a few bodies were lying around.

So had it been worse underground? And could they be walking into a battleground? Or perhaps people panicked down there when the explosions happened. She then cursed herself for not acting sooner and heading down there with the two women; safety in numbers.

'Mum, what we going to do?' her son Mathew asked, looking up at her for answers. It was the first time he had spoken for quite a while, since they had been on the move.

She tried to give him her best smile, wanting to tell him everything was going to be alright, that they were going to be with his dad in the next twenty minutes or so, that they just needed to catch a train, but the words failed her, her own confidence beginning to fail her, the madness of what she was doing, of what she had witnessed weighing heavy upon her.

She wanted to find somewhere quiet to go so she could cry.

Somewhere quiet to try to think.

'Are we going to be taking a train?' Mathew asked, still looking up at her.

She flashed him a smile, wishing she could give him a straight answer, tempted to head back to the surface, wanting to be back at the house where perhaps they could have barricaded themselves in and waited. Maybe they would have survived. Because what options there were down there seemed like suicide. As for the tunnel she was planning to head into, to risk everything in order to hope the trains were running, it just didn't seem inviting.

More suicidal.

Then her thoughts were shattered by the screams of a woman, possibly one of the suited women. The woman screamed and screamed for help. Her voice echoed, and seemed to be travelling from afar.

Her voice sent bolts of fear into Mary, who tightened her grip on her son while staring blindly in the direction of the darkened tunnels from which the cries were coming.

Then other voices could be heard, groans and growls, the woman still screaming and choking.

'Mum?' Mathew said, his voice panic-stricken, tears in his eyes.

Mary kept him close, trying to shield him again and yet felt it was only a matter of time before they would be set upon; they had been lucky so far, damn lucky.

But what could she do? And which direction would they come from?

The feeling of suffocation was stronger than ever, time slipping away, the end looming and destined to be so awful. She desperately tried to figure out how best she could save her son, but before Mary could consider anything she felt somebody tap her on her shoulder.

'Oh no,' she gasped, tears now flowing down her face. She clutched her son, too petrified to move.

'Shhh,' came a voice, the stench of alcohol hitting her.

Suddenly, she felt safe, but then thoughts of who it might be, such as a down-and-out or a scrounger, made her guarded. She cautiously turned to see a tube station worker, who looked as alarmed as she was.

He held a finger to his lips, wanting her to remain quiet, then beckoned her to follow him.

For a moment she hesitated, as she was never one to follow a stranger; she had always been careful, and had taught Mathew to be the same. And this so-called tube station worker did stink of alcohol, his clothes worn loose, and he did seem edgy and a little threatening. He had a kind of desperation about him. She had seen one two many people being attacked while on their journey to trust anyone, especially when under the influence of alcohol.

Mathew was looking up at her, wondering what they were going to do.

The tube station worker turned to face her again and said, 'Come on, hurry!'

She then recalled what she had seen and heard recently, the tunnels now quiet. Could this be her only escape? Without hesitation, she followed.

He led her to the staffroom. He had barricaded himself inside the office and the only source of light was from half a dozen candles he had lit and placed here and there, providing just enough light to see around the room. The windows were boarded up from the inside and he had used objects to reinforce the door.

Mary noticed a stale odour of sweat, tobacco and alcohol, making them choke for a brief moment. As for the room, the walls were plastered in Arsenal pictures and motorbike pictures, almost hiding a noticeboard. A desk was cluttered with personal belongings, even a leather jacket, and there was a rucksack half packed on the chair. At the far end of the room were some lockers, all of which were open, and a sink was filled with dirty cups. An open bottle of whisky sat on the sink, next to a half-filled ashtray.

Mary and Mathew glanced behind them to see the tube station worker resting his head against the door, his breathing laboured. He wiped his brow with a hankie and then ran it over his hairless head, finally turning to face Mary.

'What the fuck...' He flashed her a smile. 'Sorry, I shouldn't swear in front of the kid.' He took a deep breath and then said, 'What the hell is going on?'

Mary stared into his eyes, seeing what she felt, fear and confusion. She wished she could deliver some reassuring news, but she had been hoping he would be able to explain what was happening, perhaps even reassure her. And perhaps he would tell her if the trains were running, or would know how safe it was down there, even though the screaming of the woman told her it wasn't. Even though she knew the trains weren't running, she would not accept logic, the urge to be with her Jamie overshadowing doubt and common sense.

The tube worker attempted a reassuring smile, knowing how dazed and confused she was, that it would be a while before he would learn anything from her. He sighed, recalling what he had heard and had been through, but he had never felt this much fear in his life.

Then a minute later he glanced at Mary, flashed her a smile and said, 'By the way, the name's Ron.'

He continued to stare until she introduced herself.

'And the kid's name?' Ron asked.

'Mathew,' she answered evenly.

The lad looked around, familiarising himself with the room, which looked more like a lost property storage room, far too cluttered, or like one of his mates' bedrooms. He also noticed the boards covering the windows were game boards.

'Here you are, Mathew,' Ron said, holding out a lollipop he had produced from one of the lockers.

Mathew glanced at his mum, then the lollipop, seconds later choosing to cling to his mum rather than take it.

Taught so well.

'Thank you,' Mary said.

Ron shrugged, trying to not look too disappointed.

'Thank you for rescuing us,' Mary said.

Ron smiled and shrugged again.

'Have you any idea what's happening?' Mary asked, wondering if he knew anything, even though he had asked her if *she* knew anything.

Ron shook his head. 'People finally gone barmy. What with the recession and everything, it's been coming for a while. Just surprised it's taken this long.' He flashed her a smile. 'You witness all the mayhem down here, kind of like a pressure kettle, just expecting it to blow. Like I said, just surprised it took this long.'

Mary had flashbacks to what she had seen over the past hour, knowing for sure there was more to it than people just having a bad day. No, this was no riot. She again considered her Jamie, feeling sure he would be wondering about Mathew and her.

She hoped and prayed he hadn't decided to head home. She shook her head. No, he wouldn't be that mad, surely. Then again, perhaps he thought she wouldn't be mad enough to head for him.

People do crazy things in times of stress and she had thought that heading to Jamie would be safe.

She glanced at her surroundings again, realising how crazy she had been to risk everything. She took her mobile out of her pocket and pressed call on Jamie's number, like she had many times before. There was no signal.

'My mobile's the same, and the landline,' Ron said without taking his eyes off the two of them, wanting to say something reassuring, but unable to think of what to say.

'It's all just mad ... and where are the police?' Mary said, trying to get her head around it all, recalling the woman's screams; the endless screams she had heard, the endless slaughter she had witnessed. 'And when will it all stop?'

Ron shrugged and headed over to the sink.

'It might be wise to stay here for the night; then hopefully by the morning the rescue services may have regained control and can come and rescue us... What do you think?'

The very thought of staying with a complete stranger in a tacky little room unnerved her, especially since he had been drinking. For all she knew he could be a murderer, a paedophile.

'Listen, I can understand you having your doubts; we don't know each other and no doubt you have family you would like to reach.' He put down the whisky bottle he was about to take a sip from, held up his phone and said, 'I have been trying to contact my daughter, I'm just as anxious as you are. But I think staying here for the night would be the wisest thing to do.'

Mary thought again about her Jamie being out there, just one stop away along the tracks, just a short journey away. Well, that was if they had remained in the office. He had stated in the past that if a crisis should happen they would probably have a lockdown, so he was bound to be there.

'Are the trains still running?' she asked, knowing how pathetic it sounded, but she was going out of her mind wondering and hoped they were, so desperate to get to him.

Ron shook his head. 'Even if they were, it sounds really bad down there at the moment,' he said. 'So how about staying here for the night?' he suggested again. 'We have a foldaway mattress in one of the lockers; you two could use that.'

Before answering she considered what Jamie was doing, and imagined that he was safely barricaded in his office and having the same discussion with his colleagues, wondering how she was and trying to call her, knowing by morning they would be reunited.

'Okay,' she said finally, believing her Jamie was wise enough to do what she had thought, praying that he hadn't headed for their house in the hope they were there.

However, she was comforted by the thought that her mobile would possibly be working again the following morning, and no doubt she would be woken by message alerts. More importantly, the whole nightmare would be over. And perhaps the situation was only in Central London, and no doubt the area was being sealed off. She expected they would be woken by the police, banging on the office door, come the following day.

Ron smiled, opened his cigarette packet and offered her one, hoping she smoked, but she declined, so with a sigh he pushed them aside, got to his feet and dragged out the foldaway mattress. He gave it to Mary so she could organise it and, while she did so, tried to consider how the hell they were going to get through the night. It was going to be a very long evening, but he was sure it would have been even longer if it weren't for his two guests. He would never have made it alone all night, not with nothing but his thoughts of what he had done.

2

Day 2

KING'S CROSS TUBE STATION

7.23 a.m.

Mary had been sitting up for quite a while, watching her son sleep, looking at peace, so calm, as if what they had been through was nothing more than a movie, a kind of adventure, one that was now out of sight and mind. Mary would be occasionally distracted by Ron, who had fallen asleep in the chair, the whisky bottle at his side, his head tilted back. He was snoring, an irritating snore that sounded like a drill, getting louder, until he almost choked on his own snores. It made her feel agitated and annoyed, made her realise what a nightmare they were in. She knew she would have to be nice to him in order to prevent herself from exploding, as he was very irritating. And as for the stench in the room, it seemed to have worsened, and was making Mary feel physically sick, almost making her gag. She had prayed the police would rescue them, get them out of the hell they were in, take them far away from the room and the man they were sharing it with.

She then recalled how long the evening had seemed before they slept. Both had been talking about their loved ones, trying to find common ground, take the edginess away, though not making eye contact and often going silent when they heard a noise, hoping there would be a bang on the door and the voice of the police, but nothing. And as for their conversation, Ron had just talked about a daughter, Libby, whom he spoke of guardedly, as if he had something to hide, or perhaps they were having problems. There was no mention of any other family members. So she and Mathew had done most of the talking. And the more they had talked, the more plagued they had become with thoughts of those they cared about, the ones they had desperately tried to reach; her cousin Kelly and Jamie, her parents and her brother, whom she had tried calling, her in-laws she had also desperately tried to call. She should have been with them, not where they were right now. She knew there were so many people she would have to contact when it was all over.

And as the evening matured she had often found herself considering Ron, intrigued to know more about him.

He wasn't the best dressed and by no means best kept man, and seemed a little awkward when it came to talking about relationships, often looking for a distraction rather than saying anything. She had imagined he lived alone, and had done so for quite a while; that he had been married and had had a bad break-up, taken it badly and let himself go; that he had found it extremely difficult to get close to anybody since, even that he lived in a run-down bedsit, just on the edge of sanity, his comfort being the bottle and cigarettes, spending his spare time lost in material things, music, movies, anything rather than thinking about his problems. And obviously his two other loves were plastered all over the walls. She had imagined he pissed off most of the other employees with them, seeking attention, and he certainly had no shame when it came to the lockers, having stolen the candles from one of them, constantly keeping two burning all night, and even tampering with the smoke alarm to stop any interaction. Not only had he lost respect for himself but, it seemed to her, for everything.

She then recalled that Mathew had commented on his collection of Arsenal posters, him being a Chelsea fan and wearing his prized Chelsea shirt. They both then talked about football as if they were old friends, as if what had happened hadn't.

And as regards the night that followed, Mary had been restless, the outside world far too quiet, Ron far too noisy, and as for her dreams, they had been short, dark and disturbing. One she remembered that scared her the most was of Jamie being trapped in a building, a building which was in darkness, and all she could see was his hand, his face ... his eyes wide, face distorted, hand reaching out. Cries that ripped through her, terrifying her.

Desperately she had tried to reach for his hand, almost touching his fingers, but then his hand had pulled away. Seconds later his face was cracking, seeping with blood, crumbling, and he continued to scream and scream, and the screams were getting louder and louder, until she had jolted awake, finding herself sweating and breathing rapidly.

She had sat up, calmed her breathing and noticed Mathew was sound asleep, looking peaceful and undisturbed.

She had often stared at him, realising how much he meant to her, wondering if she had done the right thing by leaving the house; she imagined that would be the first thing the police would do, house-to-house searches.

Then the stench shook her out of her thoughts, reminding her of the hell they were in. She had wondered how on earth any woman had ever lived with the man they were sharing the room with, and wasn't surprised in the slightest that if he had been married, his wife had left him.

She glanced at Mathew again, recalling once more their desperate flight and how he had remained quiet and calm, and followed all of her instructions without a murmur – pretty grown-up for a ten year old.

Perhaps he had sensed how she was falling apart, even though she had been trying her hardest not to. He knew his mum needed him to be strong for her, a true little man in a time of crisis, a true little soldier.

She kissed him on the forehead, promising herself she would die before the boy, as his existence was all that mattered. It was a sacrifice she would be prepared to make any time.

The reason they were sat in the forsaken room.

She then thought about what she would have been doing about that time, what she had planned to do, taken for granted.

She would have been preparing breakfast for Jamie, while he grumbled about something on the news, most of which was about the recession. The Sunday papers had been quoting a possible three-day week for most. Saying how we hadn't yet had the worst, predicting a long drawn-out recession, which nobody would be able to escape. Everybody blaming the fat cats at the banks, somebody having to be strung up for the mistakes of many.

Then he would have started discussing preparations for when they would entertain his work colleagues and clients at their house, quoting how important it was that everything went smoothly and successfully. So no doubt they would have argued over something that they did not agree on, anything from the food to the time the guests would be arriving.

As a matter of fact, they had argued a lot recently and had kept their distance; it was as if they were slowly becoming strangers, but she had put it down to the stress of his job.

He would then go to work about eight, leaving her with a brief smile; not a kiss like in the old days, leaving her a little deflated and agitated, and with the task of getting Mathew ready for school, although he was pretty good when it came to being ready and organised, after which there were endless chores and tasks to be undertaken, going into the city to buy what food they needed, trying her best to operate on a budget. Jamie would more than likely call her to tell her not to forget something or tell her something else he wanted her to get, and she would probably have gone with her cousin Kelly, who would be moaning about how Jamie treated her like a doormat. Being a divorcee with two children, Kelly had a little chip on her shoulder when it came to men.

But the reality was, all that wasn't going to happen, and what made her more anxious was the fact she wasn't sure what was going to happen. And she had a gut feeling the police would not be banging on the door, as they hadn't so far, and she imagined things would get a hell of a lot worse before they got better. She even considered if it might be the end of the world, the way they had all predicted; a real-life survivor series.

But there was one thing she and Matthew so needed, and that was to be with Jamie, to know he was alright. They had got this far; only thirty more minutes away, her heart told her so. Then her immediate family would be intact.

She considered her brother again, all on his own down south. Her parents in Spain, and of course her Kelly. She had tried to reach her before heading into the city, but couldn't reach her because there were too many of those crazed people about and cars abandoned in the road, with no way through whatsoever.

Had all her family escaped it, though? Because perhaps whatever had happened had happened across the globe.

She shuddered at the thought and told herself no, it was just London.

Therefore, were they trying to contact her?

Perhaps there was a national helpline which everyone outside of London was calling. Therefore, it was only a matter of hours before the disaster was over.

Yes, she hoped, had to believe.

She checked her mobile for the hundredth time, but still no signal.

'I have to get to Jamie,' she said a little too loudly, because Ron grunted himself awake.

'Did you say something?' he asked, stretching, his voice a little hoarse.

She shook her head. 'Just thinking aloud.'

'That's one of my hazards,' Ron said, attempting a smile but yawning instead.

His head was banging thanks to the whisky, but he had needed it more than ever the previous evening, especially with what had happened and what he had seen.

He raised the less than half-empty bottle of Scotch.

'This being the other.'

'No signal yet,' Mary said, glancing at her mobile again.

Ron grunted, got to his feet and then picked up the receiver to the landline they had in the office.

'The main lines are still down as well.'

'What are we going to do?' Mary asked, looking around the little office.

The windows were boarded, they were barricaded in and the stench was so strong and bound to get worse; not forgetting she needed the use of a toilet and was sure Mathew would too upon waking.

'This might be the last place help may consider looking,' she said.

Ron nodded his agreement, rubbing the stiffness from his neck, knowing it was time to leave.

He half smiled and said, 'There is only one thing left to do.'

Mary knew what that was and was more than ready, but all the same, she waited until Ron suggested it.

'We have to leave this room and return to the surface, but I'll have a scout round first. You know, just to make sure it's safe,' Ron said.

He recalled how he had shit bricks when he had to leave the room to rescue Mary and her son from their possible fate. Then again, maybe the surface was alive with police and army personnel, or perhaps at the very least he may run in to more survivors.

Well, he hoped for one or the other.

He grabbed the whisky and took a big gulp. Dutch courage and all that. He grabbed his cigarettes, so happy to be on the move.

'I want you to lock yourself in once I leave and not to open the door unless it's me ... okay?' He spoke in a serious tone, maintaining eye contact while trying to convince himself he was doing the right thing.

Mary nodded, knowing that if anything happened to Ron it would be just her and her son; she was sure they had had luck on their side so far. And she just didn't fancy her chances of survival without Ron, because she was sure they would never have survived the night without him; and she was feeling bad now for doubting his integrity and decency, judging him for the way he looked rather than his actions, as it was actions that made a person, not looks.

Ron slipped into his worn leather jacket and picked up a torch along with an iron bar that was in his locker.

As he approached the door, Mary said, 'Do be careful.'

He glanced at her and nodded, took a deep breath, unlocked the door and stepped out of the room.

On doing so, he felt an icy shiver run through him, gripping him like a vice, possibly caused by the stillness, the darkness, the quietness or perhaps his own bravery.

He then turned on the torch and scanned the area as if he were a stranger to the place, and yet he had worked there for just under two years and practically knew the area blindfolded; it had been like a second home to him, yet he found it shocking how he could hear his own footsteps on the floor. He noticed a dead man and woman near the fare gates, where he would normally be loitering if it was a normal day. He recognised neither of them and they both smelt of decay. Then, for a brief moment, he wondered what had happened to Phil, his work colleague.

He didn't want to recall what he had done, and needed to change his thoughts and focus his mind, so he shone the torch in the direction of the tunnels leading to the trains. The tunnels were as black as space, and the torch he held seemed unable to penetrate the darkness. He then recalled the two women that had been heading in that direction, as if they had been sucked into the darkness, both destined not to return, both destined for a grizzly end. And there could be more of them waiting down there, longing for their next victims. Then he recalled the many people he had seen rushing about when it had first happened; some were crazy, and they had headed into the tunnels, others for the surface. There was bound to still be some lurking down there.

He then shone the torch in the direction of the stairs, the stairs that would take him to the surface. There was light coming from the top; the outside world was waking, and therefore he would have a chance to be spotted, hopefully by the police.

Even though he wasn't sure what would greet them on the surface, it did seem more tempting to investigate than the darkness of the tunnels. But before making a move, he had a much-needed cigarette. It might help him to relax a little, and it was a ritual he would undertake every morning, his moment to himself, just a little normality before venturing on, just like he always would.

Then, as he climbed the stairs, he decided upon having a second, helping to calm his nerves a little more, and boy, had he been aching for one for hours. He tried to imagine what he would find outside. He hoped that there was police tape everywhere, red and blue lights flashing, and yes, his daughter waiting for him, a grin on her face, racing through the police lines to hug him.

The surface, though…

There was a pale green sky.

The scene was of human decay, the stench overwhelming, and bodies as far as the eye could see, at least a hundred or more. Personal belongings scattered around them. There was a bus not far from him, blood splattered across every window, the thought of the massacre churning his stomach. There was mangled metal everywhere, metal that was once vehicles, now burnt-out shells and what looked like burnt skeletons here and there.

Shop windows smashed, their contents scattered.

Rats bathing in the blood and feeding on the rotting flesh.

Litter everywhere.

He wondered if progress was in reverse, stress and demands triggering the worst in people; broken Britain living up to its name. Well, that was how it looked to him.

Ron then became aware that some of the dead were children, clutching onto toys and mobile phones, desperate to make that final call while clinging onto something so innocent.

He looked away, not wanting to see any more, the reality so painful.

Then he heard the shuffle of feet, followed by a grunt, and it seemed to come not far from where he was standing.

He turned to face the outside world again and scanned the area, his heart racing, expecting the worst, expecting them to be staring at him.

Then he saw three or four men, all soaked in blood and sweat, clothes clinging to them, eyes wide and bewildered, faces distorted, riddled with hatred, just like the murderers he had seen down there when it all began, when he had fled for the staffroom.

They were rummaging through a car, snatching food and eating, then finally pulled a body out. There was a slight groan from the man they pulled out, and then he began screaming as they tore at his flesh with their bare hands, the crazed growling and grunting getting louder with the joy of the pain they were inflicting. Then three or four more appeared from a shop, all scouting around, looking for a victim just like the others, wanting to tear the body to pieces just like the rest.

Ron turned and headed back down the stairs, a little more eagerly than he had surfaced, the vision of those things in his mind. He hoped they hadn't seen him, not wanting to be their next victim. It was obvious from the carnage, from the dead, that they didn't care who they attacked; they would show no mercy to a coward like him.

Mary and Mathew stared anxiously as Ron entered, both eager to hear some good news.

Ron just nodded his acknowledgement, perspiration visible upon his face, distress lines on his forehead, eyes dilated. Visions of what he had seen raced though his mind. He wouldn't dream of letting them see what he had.

'Any sign of help?' Mary asked.

He shook his head, visions of the dead, visions of those that weren't dead hacking away at the dead and the almost dead, the carnage, the bloodbath, the dead children all going through his mind; a scene from hell, that's what it was, Fucking Armageddon.

'No help, none coming yet,' he managed.

He stood up straight and tried to give them a reassuring smile. He grabbed the bottle of whisky and took a sip, wanting to regain his composure, wanting to wash the thoughts from his mind. He craved another cigarette, but fought off the urge.

'So what are we going to do?' Mary asked, after giving Ron a minute or two.

Ron looked at her, then the boy. He thought about the plan he had been considering, which would be terrifying and could get them all killed, but what other options were there?

And after seeing what he had seen on the surface, they were also vulnerable while they remained where they were. It was only a matter of time until they came looking for them down there, and who knows how many there would be. He was sure the flimsy door would be no protection, and they would be destroyed in seconds. They would meet a terrifying and grizzly end, just like the poor guy they had pulled from the car.

The very thought sent him cold, and made him determined to get out.

But then the tunnels, the dark tunnels, the daunting dark looked as suffocating as quicksand, and yet he felt it was better to move in the dark than daylight, less likely to be recognised, and if they were unfortunate enough to be seen, it would be over quickly, as they wouldn't even see them coming.

He noticed Mary was waiting for a reply.

'I was thinking of making our way down the tracks. At the next junction, Euston of course, a mate of mine is on duty and in their staffroom they have a portable television and radio, as well as food. That's if he hasn't eaten it all.'

He allowed himself to smile; he would always smile whenever he thought about Barry, and he knew that if he could get to Barry they would work something out between them. They always worked well together, and would always put the world to rights when they were in the pub.

'But will he be waiting there?' Mary said, considering the possibility he had fled.

'He'll be waiting,' Ron assured her, knowing the last time they had spoken he was in the staffroom. 'If we make it, there may be more survivors, and we might hear something on the television or radio,' he said, hoping to entice them.

Mary glanced at her son, who glanced back, knowing there was a chance her husband could be there if he wasn't at the office.

'Maybe the radio and television aren't working; my iPod isn't,' Mathew said, trying to get a signal.

Ron smiled – kids and technology – and said, 'Sometimes those things don't work down here, but the portable radio never fails, kidder. So what do you think?' he asked, breaking into Mary's thoughts.

He knew if she refused he would bottle it, and it would only be a matter of time before they were found by the wrong people, and that thought terrified him.

'So there is definitely no chance of doing the journey on the surface?' she said, considering the hazards of going underground with the possibility of being attacked by those things, as well as going down there with a man she didn't even know, even though she did kind of trust him.

Ron shook his head, not wanting to tell her what he had seen, not in front of the boy.

Mary knelt down so she could look into her son's eyes and speak to him at his level.

'What do you think, Mathew? Are you going to be brave for your mum again?'

He nodded. Mary glanced at Ron and agreed.

Ron grabbed his mobile and slipped it in his pocket. He considered taking the rucksack, but didn't want the burden of carrying it, as it would slow him down with all the junk he had inside. He then grabbed the iron bar and torch, blew out the candles, turned on the torch and approached the door. Glancing back at Mary and Mathew, who were watching him, for a second or two he considered what he would do if they did meet some of those crazed people.

Would he try to save himself like before? Or would he put them first?

The words of his ex-wife echoed in his mind. *'You only care about yourself. Just as long as you're alright, that's all that matters.'*

But wasn't survival about looking after number one?

3

Day 2

KING'S CROSS TUBE STATION

8.16 a.m..

Ron paused for a moment and looked ahead at the tunnels leading to the platform, reliving the terror he felt as he saw the crowds of people racing towards him the previous day, one of the reasons for him fleeing. As the memories faded, he began to question his sanity for wanting to head in that direction. Risking his life and the lives of Mary and her son just to reach their destination, yet not knowing if Barry was waiting.

Not knowing if anybody was waiting, but possibly more of those crazed things. He then recalled his final phone call with Barry; Barry saying how mental it was there, but saying he was going to investigate what was happening. He then remembered his final words: "Oh shit, you have got to see this." And Barry had sounded shocked, kind of disturbed by what he had seen, and so he could have made a run for it.

He wouldn't have blamed him if he had; he would have done the same if he had had the bottle. And he sure wished he had, as he could have been miles away by now, possibly with his Libby.

He then considered the madness he had witnessed, the slaughter, the dead children, feeling for sure it was an end-of-the-world scenario. He even considered they may possibly be the last people on the planet.

Apart from the crazed – he was convinced they were no longer human – it was as if they were some kind of zombie, even though it sounded absurd.

But what else was Ron to think?

Surely normal, sane people wouldn't do what they had. I mean, everybody as a bad day, but not to that extent. No, they couldn't have been normal, and they definitely didn't look or act normal to Ron.

What if they were the only three normal people left?

He allowed himself to consider the possibility for a moment or two, the thought suffocating, harrowing. And he didn't have an answer or a solution as to what he would do, so, like always, he just gave up on it, pushed it to the back of his mind, rubbishing it as overreacting. He so wanted a cigarette, but chose not to, not in front of Mary and Mathew, considering it impolite, and anyway, he had only just had one while they went to the toilet. Once they were in the tunnels, the light of a cigarette could give their position away to possible predators; they would be so vulnerable then, what chance would they have? And no doubt they wouldn't be able to use the torch, well not unless it was absolutely necessary, and he would therefore have to use his instinct, as he had many a time, boasting how he could get about in the Underground blindfolded. It was time to put that theory into action.

He turned in the direction of Mary and Mathew and said, 'Let's be as quiet as we can, and stay close together.

I think the best formation of movement would be if you, Mary, place your hand on my shoulder and let me guide you both.'

She nodded, absorbing his advice, and for a moment or two he felt so proud of himself, moved by his own courage.

Ron and Mary then allowed themselves to consider what they would do if they did run into some of those things. The thought was terrifying, too terrifying to find a logical answer, though they were sure it would be hell.

Ron took a deep breath and stepped into the darkness, which quickly absorbed him and his followers. As they descended the escalators a step at a time in the direction of the platform, the atmosphere became heavier, stickier, almost dense. And as for the stench of decay, it was overwhelming, and more than anything, alarming. During their journey Ron had been tempted to use the torch, but no, not until they needed to he had told himself, so step by step they descended, even if it took forever; then again, perhaps they had forever.

Ron's breathing was laboured, his fitness certainly not up to scratch; then there were his thoughts that plagued him with possibilities of what they might run into, nothing positive, such tiring thoughts. The iron bar was slipping through his fingers and he feared letting it go because of the noise it would make.

Ron stepped on to the platform and paused, waiting for Mary and Mathew to appear at his side. They all listened hard for any signs of life, but nothing. Ron raised the torch, knowing he was going to have to use it, and he took a deep breath and finally turned it on. He carefully scanned the platform, searching every inch in a sweeping movement, from right to left, his breathing heavy. Finally, he paused the torch light on the body of a woman. They could smell the decay. He recalled her screams less than twelve hours ago, as fresh in his mind as they were then, ripping right through him, startling him, making him not want to be on his own. But there was no way she could have died down there, as the noise would not travel that far; more than likely she would have been murdered on the escalator. He shone the torch along the floor from where she lay to where they stood and noticed smears of blood. Then he turned and shone the torch up the escalator, the way they had come; again, more smears of blood. The bastards had dragged her body all the way down there, but why?

Then the thought of those crazed things still being around made him scan the platform again, but a little more slowly this time, hoping and praying they weren't nearby. His body was gripped with anxiety. Visions of what he had witnessed and heard returned to haunt him, his journey to the surface so harrowing, his mind pausing on the bloody image of those dead children. The image he knew he would never be free of, the image of the innocent being brutally murdered, for what? That image had certainly aged him.

However, the platform seemed clear. For now.

'Just wait here,' he said to Mary, not sure if what he was about to do was the right thing. But he felt an overwhelming urge to do it anyway.

He cautiously approached the dead woman's body, clutching the iron bar and torch, his imagination running wild. He imagined her trying to attack him, somehow turning into one of those things. He recalled the endless zombie films he had sat through and laughed at, now returning to haunt him with vengeance.

He paused as he got close and shone the torch from left to right, breathing heavily, expecting one of those crazed things to leap out at him, just like in the many horror films he had seen.

But nothing.

Gratefully nothing.

Unnervingly nothing.

He shone the torch on the woman; he was not sure why, perhaps just out of twisted curiosity.

Her face was grey, her eyes wide and glazed, mouth agape with dried blood around the edge. Her dark hair was matted with blood and as for the rest of her body, it had been stripped semi-naked and hacked, limbs missing and pieces of flesh torn from the torso. He glanced once more at her face, imagining the last word to have left her lips was 'why?'.

Then the stench finally hit him again, striking him four times worse than earlier. It was an overwhelming sour smell, the smell of death, ugly and unwelcoming.

Ron turned and vomited.

'Are you okay?' came Mary's voice.

'Sure,' Ron shouted back.

Then he placed his torch and weapon at his feet, slipped off his leather jacket and took off his working jacket, placing it over the woman's head, after which he muttered a prayer for her soul and asked for forgiveness for letting her down. Then, while he wrestled back into his leather jacket, he wondered where her friend was.

Wondered where her killers were.

Then again, he didn't want to hang around in case they returned, so he headed in the direction of the tracks, the only place they might have gone.

He shone his torch in both directions of the track, making sure the coast was clear, dreading what he had considered might be there. They would have more than likely headed down the tracks, possibly going after the dead woman's friend, but in which direction?

The direction they were heading in or the other? They had a fifty-fifty chance.

Not good odds, not at all.

He then shone the torch in Mary's direction, beckoning her on with his hand. She and Mathew began to heave as they approached him.

'One of the suited women, they got her, over there,' Ron said.

He chose not to shine his torch in that direction, not wanting the lad to see what he had seen, though he had probably figured out somebody had died by all the blood.

They glanced for a brief moment in the direction of the dead woman, pausing for thought, reflecting on the madness and the carnage. All asking the question they had asked many a time and would do for a long time to come – why?

Fucking why?

'I suppose we had better move,' Ron said, shining the torch on the tracks again.

'Will it be dangerous walking on the tracks?' Mathew asked.

'No, kid, the electric's down,' Ron said.

'But what if it comes on while we are down there?' Mathew asked.

Ron just smiled, knowing he would sooner die quickly than to be hacked to death and devoured by rats, like the suited woman had been, like many had been.

No sooner had they climbed down on the tracks than Ron held his hand up, letting Mary know to stop, to not move a muscle. Convinced he had heard something, but praying he was overreacting, he turned off his torch and cursed himself for using it, as he had known it would give them away.

Mary immediately pulled her son close, sensing the danger, and stared at Ron, wanting to know what was happening, wanting to know what they were going to do if it was them, yet hoping to God it wasn't.

'I'm sure I heard footsteps,' Ron whispered, listening hard, holding the iron bar even tighter.

He felt perspiration oozing out of his pores. Visions of those crazed things on the surface, the guy being dragged out of the car. The two dead near where he worked. The hacked woman behind them, her terrifying screams as they slaughtered her. The slaughtered children, all cuddling teddies and holding on to mobile phones. The red double-decker bus with the blood-splattered windows. Yes, it seemed the crazed just didn't care who they turned upon, and would definitely show the three of them no mercy. Therefore, there was possibly a huge battle ahead of them and one hell of a fight that he just didn't fancy, didn't have the stomach for. He knew who would come out on top.

'Shit,' Ron said, knowing there was more than one person approaching as the sound of shuffling feet became louder.

He recalled how they moved in groups, seeking victims in packs, like wild animals.

It was as if the darkness they had entered had lured them into a trap and boy, had he expected it. He cursed himself for being so naive, for not listening to his senses.

And how close were they? The noise could carry quite a distance, and it would still sound the same even if they were close. No chance of judging it, of knowing how long they had until they would be pounced on.

And they were possibly the same bastards who had had the suited woman. Just been waiting all along, sensing their next victim as they had stepped upon the tracks, possibly even left her body for bait; so they weren't just crazy, but canny as well, making them extremely dangerous.

But what could he do?

He glanced at the platform, the temptation so great to climb back and run like hell for the office. He did still have the half a bottle of whisky which he could enjoy, not forgetting the cigarettes, and also some 'Who' on his MP3 player. He would have a swell time before those things murdered him. At least then death would be less painful, although he so didn't want to die alone. But what about Mary and her son? They wouldn't stand a chance.

No, he couldn't leave them, couldn't bear hearing them screaming and crying as he ran; no amount of whisky could erase that.

And he wasn't that inhuman, even though that bitch of an ex-wife thought he was.

He looked at Mary, wondering how best to save her and Mathew if this turned out to be what he feared. He knew it was too late for them to climb back up on the platform. And he didn't have time to think in detail, as a quick plan was needed, so he whispered to them to go back, and if anything should happen to run like hell. At least they would be heading in the direction of Euston, and may have a chance if they were quick enough.

As for him, he wasn't sure.

Perhaps he would fight...

Or climb back up on the platform and run for the staffroom. He could try to get those crazed things to follow him, as he was sure even though he wasn't all that fit he could outrun them; it was surprising what energy you could find when gripped by fear. That would definitely give Mary and Mathew a chance.

'Be careful, Ron,' Mary whispered, just before she retreated into total darkness.

He flashed her a smile, proud for a second or two of his own bravery, realising the fight it was to be. He would go out with a bang, prove to the world he could fight when the time came, even though the world would never witness it, would never know. Then again, why should he care about the world witnessing it, apart from his Libby? It's not like anybody else ever cared about him. So he wiped the perspiration from his forehead and stepped forward, heart beating fast, clenching the iron bar and torch. Suddenly, he felt torn between whether he was doing the right thing or not.

The platform looked welcoming.

So welcoming.

But he remained focused, aimed the torch in the direction he had heard the footsteps and, before he turned it on, tightened his grip on the iron bar, knowing he'd probably only have a split second to act if it came to the worst.

And if there were more than two, he was going to have to act extremely fast.

But he was ready, his adrenalin revving.

He waited for the sound of the footsteps getting louder, which they did, but they had slowed down, as if they had sensed his presence, preparing themselves for the battle.

Preparing themselves to pounce.

He gritted his teeth and muttered, 'To hell with it, here goes.'

He hit the button to turn on the torch, to be met immediately by the light of another torch.

'WHO THE FUCK ARE YOU?' Ron shouted, getting ready to pounce, blood pumping hard and fast.

'WHO THE FUCK ARE YOU?' came a reply.

Ron froze for a moment, confused, then realised it had to be somebody civilised since they were talking and not pouncing. So he sighed, stood up straight, wiped the perspiration from his brow, looked towards the heavens and said, 'Thank God there are other people.'

'The feeling's mutual,' came the voice.

The person then approached Ron, the torchlight shining in his face. Ron became aware that the man was a police officer, with two other people in tow.

He was tall and slender, his face slightly weathered, and he had a crew cut and looked sharp. He appeared calm, in control. Not like Ron, who was almost in pieces.

'How many of you are there?' the officer asked, his face serious, eyes darting from left to right.

'Just two more; Mary, and her son Mathew,' Ron replied, pointing in their direction.

The officer shone his torch in that direction and saw their faces, both terrified.

Ron held his hand out and said, 'And I'm Ron.'

'John,' the officer said, briefly shaking his hand, shining the torch at their feet.

John glanced at the two people behind him, a male and female, both dressed in creased tracksuits that were dirty and looked worn, both looking edgy.

'This is Jake and Emma. Met them late last night, hiding; couldn't blame them.'

They all shared a brief smile.

John glanced at Ron. 'So whereabouts are you heading?'

'Going for Euston,' Ron said. 'What about you?' he asked, dabbing his forehead with some tissue he had produced from a pocket.

John glanced at the platform. 'We have come down from Islington and were planning on exiting here, but take it it's not good?'

'It's a little rough up on the surface, loads of those mad fuckers about, worth avoiding,' Ron said, hoping he had persuaded them to join them; the more there were of them, the more they had a chance of staying alive.

'Well…' John said, considering the journey they had made along the tracks, which had been hazardous and hard going. He had planned to exit there and head for St Pancras to steal a taxi, which should get him where he intended to go, where he so needed to go. As for the other two, he couldn't give a shit.

He glanced at the young couple he had for company, then at Ron and his company. They seemed genuine, caring people, and he knew they could all get themselves killed without him, who at least had a gun, and he had seen enough death without seeing any more, or having any more deaths on his conscience.

'I suppose we should stay together … safety in numbers,' John said, not wanting to make any promises or commitment though. *Just get to the next junction, get them all to some kind of safety, then assess the situation from there on.*

'Sure,' Ron said, smiling, grateful for the support.

He knew, though, that the killers of the suited woman had more than likely gone the way they were about to head, and could be waiting in the dark.

Just waiting.

And yet he felt calm, the sight of the gun the officer was holding helping him feel at ease, although he decided to keep this to himself. But he would listen hard, be ready to inform him if the time should come.

John glanced at the iron bar Ron was holding.

'I take it that is your only source of protection?'

Ron nodded, relaxing his hand as he realised he was still gripping on to it.

'And is there any particular reason why you're heading to Euston? I feel going further back into the city centre may be dangerous, possibly worse than what you are leaving behind,' John said, taking his baton out of its holding compartment.

Recalling the action he had seen, he was not too eager to head back in that direction. Last time he had been with three hundred of his colleagues and they still didn't stand a chance, so what chance would they have if they ran into a bunch of those things? And like before, there could be a hell of a lot waiting for them.

'A mate of mine, Barry, he should be there, and they have an office with a healthy supply of food and drink. Not forgetting a radio and television,' Ron said, hoping it was enough to tempt the officer to go with them, knowing those murderous bastards didn't have a chance while John had the gun.

'Sounds sensible to head in the direction you have suggested,' John said, and gave his baton to Ron. 'More effective than the iron bar.'

Ron thanked him, then offered the iron bar to Jake.

'Shall we make tracks?' John said, eager to get moving, since there would be so much to do upon reaching their destination.

Ron agreed, as did the others.

John and Ron were to lead, with Jake and Emma at the rear, and Mary and Mathew in the middle. Before they started their journey along the tracks, Ron produced the lollipop from his pocket and offered it to Mathew again, who now gratefully accepted, but not before saying, 'I wouldn't normally take lollipops from an Arsenal supporter.'

They shared a smile, appreciating a little humour in such dark times.

They all walked along the tracks for what seemed like forever, feeling unattached from everyone else within their small band, all remaining silent, pausing every now and then when they heard noises, praying it wasn't one of those crazed people. All expecting it to be them, especially Ron, and all considering what they would do if one or perhaps more appeared, feeling for sure it would be blind panic; the security of the gun meant nothing in the darkness, they may even end up with one of their party being shot by accident.

When the panic ceased and they returned to their normal thoughts, they all considered what they would have been doing if what had happened hadn't, reflecting on what they would have done twenty-four hours ago if they had known what they knew now. Then they considered what they wanted to do on reaching their destination, all planning their own little things that were so important to them.

Flicking from the future, to the past, to the present as fast as a candle would flicker.

And as they travelled, it seemed the darkness around them was as suffocating as their thoughts, the stagnant air as heavy as their limbs, and yet all with so many regrets, so much uncertainty. So much they needed to know...

Suddenly, Ron stopped. Gripping John's forearm, he said, 'The station is just ahead.'

He felt for sure the killers would be there, waiting, just waiting to pounce, like they had waited for the suited woman.

John turned and switched on his torch, shining it at their feet, and said, 'Ron and I will go ahead and check things out, and if anything should go wrong, I shall use the gun. That will be the indication for the rest of you to head back as quickly as you can... Is that okay with everyone?'

They all nodded, briefly glancing at each other, gripped with anxiety. All considering what their best course of action would be if it were all to go wrong. Knowing their band would disintegrate and it would no doubt be a battle of the fittest.

Blind panic returned.

All hoping and praying it wouldn't come to that; no, it mustn't come to that. They had almost convinced themselves it was only a matter of time.

Ron flashed a smile at Mary, then winked at Mathew, offering them courage and support. They both smiled back, which gave Ron courage, and then he followed John.

'I'll go first,' John said, trying to sound sure and confident, but knowing if a paper bag moved it would unnerve him; he'd probably even shoot at it.

He climbed up onto the platform and scanned the area using the torch, gun ready in the other hand.

There were two dead bodies ahead, litter scattered everywhere, the odd rodent's eyes glowing, but no sign of human life apart from the obvious dead. No sign either of any of the mad people. He then shone his torch in the direction of Ron and beckoned him on.

They both crept across the platform, both expecting the worst with each step they took. Taking a look at the two dead as they passed them, they failed to recognise the men in suits, but then they had never expected to; it was just a force of habit. They both tensed on their approach to the stairs, worse scenarios rushing through their minds, expecting to be jumped on.

Ron was thinking about the suited woman, and wondered if the two men had been butchered by the same people, possibly trying to track down her friend; predator after prey. The thought sent him cold.

And where was her friend?

Had she made it to safety, or had they finally caught up with her?

On reaching the escalator, John cautiously shone the torch along the flight, dreading what they may see, and noticing smears of blood that told the story of some souls' desperate flight for the stairs, trying to escape the nightmare. Ron was so tempted to tell John about the suited woman, about the possibility of the crazed somewhere nearby, but chose not to.

John and Ron shared a glance before climbing the escalators, both filled with anxiety as regards what they could be walking into, both recalling the frightening events they had witnessed.

Traces of blood continued right to the top and on to the next set of steps, heading in the direction of the ticket booths and office.

Ron thought of Barry.

Had he tried to save someone on the platform? Had he tried to save as many as he could, helping them to the staffroom?

And were they there now, all snuggled in the office, all toasting to their hero, their saviour?

Ron froze as he saw a familiar person lying face down near the staffroom, thoughts of pity overwhelming him.

John shone the torch in the direction and saw the body of a large man. He lay in a pool of his own blood, his right hand clutching an iron bar, knuckles pure white.

'That a mate of yours?' John asked Ron.

'Barry,' Ron said, pausing in front of him.

John patted him upon his shoulder. 'Sorry, mate.'

'I have seen some terrible things so far, but you don't realise how cruel the situation is until you see one of your best mates lying dead, do you?' Ron said, still staring at Barry, the times they had had together returning thick and fast.

John nodded his agreement. He had been there more than once, and the memories were painful.

Ron slipped off his leather jacket and placed it over Barry's head, whispering the words, 'Rest in peace, big man.'

Visions of countless times they had shared together returned again, thick and fast. They were blissful times, times they thought would never end, never, not the way they had.

A moment of silence then passed between Ron and John, both reflecting on separate tragedies they had witnessed in less than twelve hours. However, their moment was shattered by a noise coming from the office, like somebody shuffling around, possibly the one that had killed Barry, or somebody he was trying to protect.

John glanced in the direction of the staffroom, gripped the gun he was holding and cautiously approached. The torch he was holding was now switched off.

He paused at the entrance to the office, the door slightly ajar, firmly holding the trigger, plucking up the courage to carry out the manoeuvre he was about to undertake.

He had done it endless times in training and it always came easy, but it took such a lot of concentration and guts when it came to the real thing.

He took a deep breath and then, in the blink of an eye, John found himself aiming the gun straight at a woman sat on the floor.

For a second or two he just stared into the startled woman's eyes, trying to decide if she was one of the deranged people.

'Please,' she said, and he lowered the gun, noticing she was bleeding from her leg and had lost a lot of blood.

He immediately shouted for Ron to enter.

'Will there be a first aid kit in here?' John asked Ron as he entered.

'Sure,' he said, switching on his torch and rummaging through a cupboard, producing a first aid box a minute or two later.

John took it from him and then asked Ron to bring the rest of the group to the room.

When he had left, John applied his first aid skills to the woman without speaking, finding himself thinking about the many other people the previous evening who had needed his assistance but he had failed to help. He had let people down, including one special person, and that thought hurt like hell. If anything had happened to her, he just wasn't sure what he would do.

Minutes later, they all entered the room and Ron closed the door behind them. Ron then helped John get the woman to her feet and seated upon a chair, after which she introduced herself through gritted teeth as Lisa.

The rest of the party briefly introduced themselves, after which John glanced at Ron and said, 'The radio and television?'

Ron was staring at Lisa and didn't answer, recalling who she was, feeling responsible for her injuries, for the death of her friend, visions of her friend so fresh in his mind, her screams still cutting through him.

'You're wasting your time, there is no electricity,' Lisa said, the pain evident on her clammy white face.

'Ron?' John said, staring at Ron.

'Oh yes,' Ron said, snapping out of his thoughts, the visions fading briefly.

'They're battery operated as well,' Ron stated. He went through the cupboards for batteries, but there weren't any.

'Damn,' John said.

'So what do we do now?' asked Jake, the youth who had hardly spoken since joining Ron's party.

'You said something about food?' John said to Ron.

He nodded, went through another cupboard and produced crisps, biscuits and a two-litre bottle of warm pop. He turned and smiled as he showed his gains, finally proud to have made the trip worthwhile, credibility in tact.

They all sat around in silence and ate, handing round the pop, wondering where they should go from there, what their plans were.

John had planned to exit at this stage, hoping to walk into a room full of other survivors, one or two other tube staff, maybe even a transport police officer amongst them. If they'd been strong enough for him to leave, he would have headed for the surface, probably straight for the train station, telling them he would send for help, but first he'd get himself a cab and head for Debbie. But the reality was that there was the woman with the child who looked so anxious, the injured woman who looked confused, the young couple who he couldn't trust and of course the tube worker who was falling apart, and all of them had kind of looked up to John, respected him for being the law. His duty was to look after them, look out for them and get them to safety. They needed him, especially with the dead out there; no doubt trouble wasn't too far away, and boy, did he know how dangerous those things were. Yes, they needed him and he was sure they could do with his help. He could therefore gain some much-needed respect again, and erase some demons that had recently formed.

As for Ron, he was hoping this stop would be his terminal, him and Barry sitting it out until the situation passed. He would then venture out and find his daughter, imagining his Libby was safe, living in north-east London, where it was possibly not as bad. But no, that wasn't to be, life was never that easy, it never had been for him; every time he had made a plan in his life it had dissolved before his eyes, bad luck seeming to follow him everywhere. And right there and then he was happy to hang out with the rest of them for the time being, hoping they would all stick together, but more than anything he hoped his daughter was safe, wished he had taken the chance when he had it and headed for her rather than barricade himself in the office, and he prayed he wouldn't have to live to regret that.

Mary wanted to be with her husband, and was aware of the huge risk she would have to undertake. She may have to go on alone with her son, but she was sure it would pay off, as he only worked a ten-minute walk away. She had a strong feeling he was there, waiting for her, just waiting. And the very thought of him waiting gave her itchy feet, that urge to move, and she could not stand sitting around in another office again, not without Jamie.

Lisa wasn't in a fit state to go anywhere fast and was more than happy to remain where she was. She had so much going through her mind and knew she could very easily fall to pieces, finding it hard to remain strong, especially after what she had seen and done, been through. She had never thought in her wildest dreams she would ever feel so much mental and physical pain. Yes, remaining where she was, was definitely the best form of action for her.

As for Jake and Emma, they were just happy to tag along for now...

'What's going to be the next move?' Jake asked, breaking the silence, asking the question on everybody's mind, wondering if they were going to work together or split.

'As you are probably all aware, there are only two options for us,' John said, making sure he had everyone's attention. 'We either continue along the Underground, or head for the surface. We obviously need to find a rescue camp or something, and there are bound to be some.'

'We would definitely be better on the surface,' Jake said, recalling the nightmare journey they had undergone to get where they were, fumbling along the tracks, almost slipping and breaking their necks, cursing each step along the way. So many dreads in their minds, from worrying about being jumped by those things to the possibility the tracks would come alive again.

'That's what everybody thought yesterday. It was like a mass exodus down here when it happened, but now there are dead everywhere,' Ron said, knowing if the surface was anything like what he had witnessed at King's Cross, their survival would be in question.

'But there are bound to be police and army about. We are more likely to be rescued up there than down here, and it's no good locking ourselves in here and waiting for them to come knocking,' Jake said. 'For all we know, it might all be over.'

'Why don't we get batteries for the radio?' Mathew asked, playing with it having taken it out of the open cupboard.

John and Ron shared a look, knowing there were plenty of shops on the surface, and it would give them a chance to scout around.

Ron winked at Mathew and said, 'Good idea, kid. It's a good job we have you on-board.'

Jake looked from Ron to John, then back again, wanting an explanation; they all wanted an explanation.

'Ron and I will head for the surface. There's plenty of shops up there, and we'll see what we can salvage. It'll also give us a chance to see if there is any help about,' John stated.

'And while we are gone, make sure you lock the door and don't open it unless we say it's us,' John said, glancing at them all.

'I'll come too,' Jake said, getting to his feet, a sly smile on his face. 'Could do with the fresh air, and a cigarette.'

John nodded, then glanced at the three women and the boy and said, 'Remember, lock the door.'

All four agreed, after which John led his party out. Ron was at the rear and glanced at Mary and Mathew, flashing them a smile before reassuring them they would be as quick they could. He gave them his torch, as the room was pretty dark.

On stepping out of the room they were greeted with the familiar darkness and a stench of human decay that seemed as heavy as the stagnant air, Barry reminding them he was there, as well as the other victims.

Before reaching the surface, John and Ron decided to give Barry a little dignity by moving his body and finding an area to lay him to rest. Ron said a few words in honour of him, after which he offered the two men a cigarette. All three stood smoking, reflective, and then pushed on without saying a word, all wanting to throw up as the stench remained heavy, but not daring to in front of the others.

They climbed the stairs leading to the surface, maintaining silence. The daylight became brighter, welcoming, yet all felt a sense of dread as they approached, wondering what they would do if they were met by some of those crazed people.

All feeling for sure that once more they were going to be on their own when it came to getting out of the situation, because isn't everybody out to look after number one when it comes to mortal danger? And boy, they had all witnessed selfish behaviour within the past twenty-four hours.

That was the reason they had managed to stay alive.

They paused as they reached the surface and stared out into the world before them.

Bodies lay all along Euston Road, in front of shops, takeaways, public houses, grand buildings, all with their windows shattered, most of their contents spilled upon the streets. Though there were shops that had the steel shutters down, in the vicinity of the station, the owners wise enough to use them before fleeing. And yet the green eerie smog was still rising from the drains, still in the air.

From where they stood, Euston Square looked like a battleground, with cars mangled with other cars, bodies flung from them or dragged out; either way, they were all butchered.

There was litter dancing around the bodies, performing a kind of ritual dance around the dead.

'This country is seriously fucked up,' Jake said, trying to take in what they were witnessing.

He suddenly crouched down and picked up a portable camera he had spotted lying next to the body of a pretty blonde lady.

They all watched in silence as he played the content.

It showed a woman sitting at a table, possibly outside a coffee shop, a hot beverage in her hand and a huge smile on her face, her long blonde hair glistening in the sun, eyes sparkling, smiling her best at the cameraman who was speaking to her in French, asking her to smile and encouraging her to say something, the sun streaking every now and then across the camera, the lady laughing, talking and continuing to smile; a face that was made for the camera, so magnetising, she was certainly enjoying every golden moment, *their* special moment. This playful scene went on for five minutes, which Jake forwarded. Then there was thick green smog, the sound of choking, a woman's voice in French asking if he was alright, her voice serious, concerned, asking what on earth was happening and beginning to choke herself; then moments later, the camera fuzzed as it hit the ground, yet the woman's screams could still be heard. And she continued to scream until she began to gargle.

'Listen!' Ron interrupted.

John and Jake glanced at him, startled, and Jake switched off the camera.

Suddenly, they all heard it, the sound of beating that got louder and was now overhead. They all looked up to see a police helicopter, which had a camera and a PA system that kept repeating the message: *All survivors head for Parliament Hill, all survivors head for Parliament Hill.* Then it disappeared from sight.

'We could have waved or something,' Jake said.

'Our own safety comes first,' Ron said, not wanting to look too conspicuous, unsure who was watching. Anyway, they were asking them to head for Parliament Hill, make their own way there.

'Let's get moving, eh?' John said, heading in the direction of the shops, not wanting to hang around, as he still had visions of the horrors he had witnessed. The camera had also creeped him out.

Jake placed the camera back where he had found it, next to the woman on the film, and stared at it for a brief moment, knowing she would no longer need it. It was an expensive camera, possibly worth one hundred pounds. Then he followed the others upon hearing John calling him.

They headed for the nearest shop they could find which would sell what they were looking for. The door was bashed to bits, as if whoever had owned it had barricaded themselves in, in the hope it would be enough protection.

John then recalled the riot shields locked together, the brute force of three hundred police behind them. They smashed through them in seconds, so what chance did a flimsy door have? He then considered the flimsy door protecting the other four in the Underground and knew they had to hurry back, just in case.

As they entered the shop, they had to step over a dead woman's body. Her face was distorted with terror, mouth agape, eyes wide, her final moments on earth being of blind panic and confusion; a victim like so many of a mindless slaughter.

Ron patted John on his back, encouraging him to look away. Then as they glanced in the direction of the counter they stared straight into the eyes of a dead man slumped over it, one arm frozen out as if he had tried to prevent something or been crying out for help; every dead person would have a tale to tell, but there was no one to hear them. Their voices silenced, a crime in itself.

'The place sure has been trashed,' Jake said, glancing around at the shop's contents strewn across the floor, broken glass crunching underfoot. He began snatching cigarettes and chocolate bars.

John and Ron shared a look, but chose not to say anything, knowing unity was going to be their strength; they would definitely need each other if they were to survive. They were all wondering if they should have chanced it and tried to flag down the helicopter.

John picked up a packet of batteries that would fit the radio, glanced at Jake who was still scavenging and said, 'We'd better be going, mate, just in case…'

'Shit!' Ron interrupted, standing near a broken window.

'What is it?' John asked, glancing in his direction, heart beating madly.

'Just get down,' Ron said, crouching, his face covered in perspiration.

John did as he said, waiting for an explanation.

Ron peered out of the broken window and indicated what he was looking at with his index finger. John crept to his side, trying not to make too much noise.

There was a man with a posture of someone from days of old, days of primitive. He had a wild look on his face and was glancing around, as if he had sensed their presence.

It was the same sort of posture and actions of many he had witnessed and had fought against, but had lost control of the city to within minutes – one hell of a powerful opponent.

'Shoot him,' Jake said, opening one of the packets of cigarettes.

John shook his head, glanced at Jake and said, 'But there may be more of them. And I wouldn't fancy our chances against loads of those things.'

'He's gone,' Ron interrupted.

John and Jake both glanced out of the window, noticing he was no longer there.

'Where did he go?' John asked.

Ron thumbed to the right. 'Down Euston Road.'

'Then let's go, eh, before he comes back,' John said.

Nobody complained.

Jake offered them both a cigarette and they accepted without hesitation.

Ron entered the office first, holding the batteries up. He flashed a smile at Mathew and then tossed them over to him. Mathew undid them and placed them in the radio. They all sat in silence while he tried to tune in a station, but all they got was interference.

'So what's it like on top?' Mary asked, eager to know something.

'Pretty bad,' Ron said. He tried a smile and then said, 'There was a police helicopter in the air, so they must suspect survivors, and they were advising us to head for Parliament Hill.'

Mary nodded, feeling for sure Jamie would be alright. His office block was only minutes away and she was sure he would be there.

'But we can't go walking around office blocks hoping to bump into survivors, we might bump into the wrong sort,' John said, no intention of hunting down people for the sake of it.

'So we have to make it to Parliament Hill,' Ron stated, trying to sound optimistic. He hoped Libby was there, realising they weren't too far away.

John nodded, wondering how on earth they would be able to without running into more of those things, especially with them being in the heart of the city.

The Underground?

Or take a chance on the surface?

'We either chance it on the surface or walk the lines to another station; either way, we need to find some transport,' John said, stating the obvious, though he knew what a killer it was to walk the lines, and this time they had an injured woman with them, and the further they went into the city, the worse it would more than likely be.

'At least we didn't run into any of those things down here, and Warren Street station isn't too far,' Ron said.

'But we might not be so lucky next time,' Jake stated. 'And I don't fancy meeting any of those things in those dark tunnels; it would be a massacre.'

'But they would only come at us head-on or from behind, and we do have ammunition and other weapons,' Ron said, trying to convince himself as much as the others, though recalling how petrified he had been down there.

'Let's forget about the worst-case scenarios and concentrate on how best we should travel. We need the safest route to finding transport,' John said.

'Suppose if we hit the surface, there is a chance the helicopter may come over again and spot us. Maybe then they will send us some help,' Mary said, preferring the surface option.

'And if we stay down here, where will we head? And who's to say it's going to be any better? And it killed us getting here,' Jake said, feeling for sure the surface was their best option, even though one of those things was scouting around up there.

'Couldn't we just take the chance and wait here, perhaps see if help reaches us? She is really badly hurt and we would have to carry her,' said Emma, Jake's girlfriend, referring to Lisa's predicament. It was the first time she had spoken in present company.

'But she requires emergency treatment, and may deteriorate down here,' Jake said, nudging Emma, wanting her to support his idea.

'Thanks for reminding me,' Lisa said through gritted teeth.

They again considered their options.

'There is only one sensible thing to do,' Ron said.

They all looked at him, eager to know his plan.

'Perhaps two of us could scout down the lines, check out the next station and see if there is any means of transport that way, and if it's a no go, then perhaps we could hit the surface when it's dark, move under cover, head into the train station or perhaps one of the bus stations,' Ron said.

'Sounds like a great idea,' John said.

The others all agreed.

'How about you and me, Jake?' John said.

'Okay,' Jake said, sounding unsure, not looking forward to another daunting journey along the tracks.

And while Jake went over to Emma, Ron went over to John.

'Are you sure about taking him with you, because any sign of trouble and he will be away?' Ron said.

'I know, but these women need one of us, and Mary and her son seem close to you,' John said. 'And no disrespect, Ron, but the kid looks fitter than you. We both have a better chance of survival.'

Ron smiled. 'Okay, mate, just be careful, and any sign of trouble, just get out of there.'

'We will,' John assured him.

Ron then explained the tunnel system. As John and Jake left, Ron locked the door behind them. He wondered if they would see them again, but knew they had to remain confident and pray they would return with good news.

He turned to face the others and said, 'How about if we all properly introduce ourselves, explain where we were before this all happened? And how we managed to be where we were when we met? Perhaps then we may gain some sort of insight into what happened.'

They all agreed. They all had a story to be told, yet were plagued with so many demons that longed to come out.

To spill out.

4

RON'S STORY

'I was to start duty round about three, but I always have a habit of cutting it fine, especially when it comes to the afternoon shift. You see, afternoon shifts are the worst, as they are neither here nor there. Tend to get in the way of your life. Smack in the middle of a day, so fucking inconvenient. Then again, I do try to make the most of the two halves. First half starting with breakfast at the Wetherspoons. I'd meet up with a few mates, often Barry would be one of them; the benefit of twenty-four-hour drinking, I would down a few with breakfast. We'd have a right good laugh, talk about the soccer, about the weather, anything really. And have the odd moan about this and that, mostly how we aren't allowed to smoke in pubs any more. Then there was the hot topic of the recession, killing the pub industry, and the crying shame of how nobody wants to do anything about it. Long gone are the days when you'd walk in and feel a great atmosphere. No, you will never see those days ever again, not even when all this is over.'

He paused and smiled, realising how he was ranting away as if he was in the pub. Then he continued.

'And once our banter and breakfast was over, we would all go our own way, feeling ready to face the world, our little therapy session over. I'd usually head back to the flat and put on some music, as I only live round the corner from the Wetherspoons. And as regards music, I am listening to a little Who at the moment; a little before my time, but still a great band. You know, just kind of sitting around, with music, cigarettes and coffee, kind of old-age rock and roll. Just waiting for dinner time, then time to get ready and all that. And yesterday, just like most days, I had about two or three text messages from my daughter. She would always text me round about ten-ish, wanting a favour or scrounging money.'

Ron paused, thinking about his daughter, wondering if she was alright, because deep down the thought of her being out there somewhere terrified him. Even though she made out she was big and strong, in his eyes she would always be his little girl, his little Libby. But those she lived with would never look out for her in the crisis they were in; no, they were nothing but a bunch of selfish bastards. Then again, she did kind of remind him of himself when it came to survival. He was confident she had survived – a born survivor like him. Or perhaps he was kidding himself, just to find an excuse why he hadn't had the bottle to try to reach her.

'Yes, she wanted some money off me. She would always complain about how her mum never gave her anything. Recently, she said she had even refused to call her or answer her phone calls, practically disowned her own daughter.' He smiled. 'I don't have a great deal of money, but I would always give her what she needed, even if I have to go short. Things you do for your children, eh?'

He then recalled racing across the city on his motorbike, through red lights and almost hitting a pedestrian or two, being ranted at and having fists shaken at him, car horns screaming at him, letting him know of another close shave he had survived. The beer he had had still in his system making him a little daring and reckless, making him feel like Steve McQueen. And on reaching her so-called home, a run-down three-storey house she shared with half a dozen lowlifes, she was waiting for him, looking a little disappointed because he was late, arms folded, foot tapping. He could never understand her urgency for the money, but she would always be waiting outside. He knew on giving it to her, her face would light up and he would receive a hug. But how thin she was; suppose she takes after her mother in that way. Though Ron would cherish that hug and smile, take it as a positive vibe, daughter still needing her father, the same look he had cherished and had made him feel so complete as a younger man when his Libby was a child made him feel as if he could face anything life chose to throw at him. He then recalled her so-called housemates. Every time he dropped by they would be watching from behind the grubby lace that hung at the windows, as if it was entertainment to them, sniggering away. The thought angered him, so he continued with his story.

'Well, back to the subject of work. Like I said, I would always cut it fine getting to work, and especially yesterday, with visiting my daughter. And anyway, all you ever get down here is hassle, and if it isn't from the miserable commuters it's from the supervisor and his arse-licking mates. Phil's his name, the supervisor that is; boy, is he an old misery, and boy, does he hate the way

I decorate the staffroom, moaning about Health and Safety and all that rubbish. Always banging on about when my contract was up how there was no way they would renew it.'

Ron then recalled the way his so-called work colleagues would talk behind his back, Phil and his arse-lickers, all wanting him out, giving him the crap jobs to do, the hassle. Many a time Ron had complained to Barry, the Union Steward, and he had got Ron out of a few scraps. Ron admired him for that.

'Well, the hours leading up to the explosion and madness was busy as usual. Barry had text me a few times, asking me if I was sober enough to work, as I did have more than I normally would that morning. And he had made comments on the bottle of whisky I had smuggled in to work. I always like a little in my coffee when it gets really cold. Does help to keep me chilled, though I have to be so careful, as Phil was aching to test me, get rid of me as soon as possible.' He smiled. 'Don't worry, not all the tube staff are like me. I'm a kind of one-off. A kind of rebel... Well, maybe Barry was as well, though it was me who corrupted him.'

Ron smiled, remembering his deceased buddy, the fond memories of the times they had had together and the personal tragedies that had brought them together, the tragedies that had bonded their friendship. And although Ron had many friends, Barry was his closest, the one who knew what it was like to go through what he had. From having everything to almost nothing. What it was like to be alone and cry yourself to sleep, wondering why their lives were so jinxed. Yes, he would have hit rock bottom if it weren't for his daughter and his good mate Barry. And it was Barry who had got him the job at the Underground. Before that he had been a security guard on nights, and was expecting to return to security again, as there was no way he was going to keep his job down there.

'Barry was like me, a forty-something divorcee … both of us with long-term failed marriages behind us… Guess we were like the likely lads, but don't get me wrong, we both kind of wished we could meet the right one, get back into a relationship, but it just seems as if modern relationships are all or nothing, no breathing space. And boy, there are plenty of head games to play along the way. If modern love is about going insane then I want out all together. Well, that was the impression I got from the few dates I had had. So, apart from Libby, it was to be beer, bikes and Arsenal. Not forgetting my music as well. Yes, two ageing men acting badly.'

He again allowed himself to smile, thinking of the endless binges they had been on, both always the last remaining when all others had gone home and both having cynical minds when it came to authority.

Ron's face then hardened as he recalled his mate lying face down, recalled their final conversation. Not the jolly occasion they had often joked about when they would comment on the final curtain descending and the things they had often talked about when staggering back to the flats after a bender.

'Like I said, there was nothing happening. Then the explosion that rocked the Underground shook us all to the ground. I immediately text Barry, asked him if he was fine and if he knew what had happened. I mean, I guess like everybody else I was expecting it was a terrorist. Then suddenly, there were people screaming and running around everywhere, fucking mad Phil trying to give out orders, some of his arse-lickers following them, others just running for it. As for me, I was still in shock. Well, Barry called me, said he was in the staffroom and advised me to do the same. It was then that I noticed these crazed people attacking folk. So without hesitation I raced for the staffroom. I just don't know what was the most terrifying, the explosion or the way people were reacting.'

Ron paused, reflecting on the whole event. It all seemed to happen so fast; one minute he was standing there, bored as hell, then he was thrown to the ground. The noise, the screams, the flashes of butchery, all blurring into one and cutting right through him, leaving him petrified, too scared to do his job. Then, on receiving Barry's advice, the encouragement he needed, he ran for the staffroom and locked himself in, waiting for Barry to text him or call him again. Barry called him a few moments later, saying how mental it all was and how he was going to check things out. Ron recalled telling him not to, and then heard Phil banging on the door, begging him to open it, begging him to let him in, but all he could think of was saving himself, so he barricaded himself in. He just had a brain freeze, and didn't even have the nerve to call his daughter. He was sweating and falling apart. And when the second explosion happened, he just sat with his head in his hands, trembling and crying.

He then reflected on how brave Barry had been, not wanting to think about the dilemma he found himself in.

Perhaps he didn't really know Barry as well as he had thought, as he had imagined him to be a coward like himself. But how wrong he was. No, Barry had been battling it out with those things like a true hero, while he was frantically boarding up the windows and barricading the door, head fuzzing and trembling, on the verge of a breakdown.

'I can still remember his very last words the final time I spoke to him... He said, "Oh shit, you have got to see this."'

The words echoed in Ron's mind and had done ever since seeing his mate.

'And after barricading myself in, I just sat there trying to get my mobile working again, but there was no signal, and text wasn't working either. And the landline was down... I felt isolated, scared. I must have been sitting there for ages, thinking of what could possibly be happening, but too scared to take a look, far too scared to do my job. So I opened the bottle of whisky, put on my MP3 player and listened to the Who while I smoked and drank. Just shut the world out, hoping it would all go away... I buried my head in the sand, giving nobody, nothing a thought, just wanting to escape reality, expecting the police to come bursting through the door, me kissing goodbye to my shitty job, but no, that didn't happen.

'Then, after a little Dutch courage and wrestling with my conscience, I went through the other lockers. I know I shouldn't have done, but I was desperate for a distraction, to see what I could find; candles, food... I was just really hungry and desperate for light, as I was in the dark apart from the torch I had. I was stealing people's stuff and boy, did I feel low. I just regret not making a move when it first happened, to try and reach my daughter... But no, I told myself it was just the Underground that had gone mad, convinced myself it was just the Underground. Convinced myself it was some crazy gang gone barmy, probably a prison outing or something lame. I found myself wondering more than once if I was in hell. Then, when it all went quiet, I opened the door and glanced out to see two women racing past the office. I was going to go out to them, but they were gone like a shot, steaming straight into the darkness. It was then I realised it must be as bad out there as it was down here... Had me thinking again, falling apart again.'

He then recalled closing the door again, the screams of that woman terrifying him. He was going to make a run for it, but on opening the door he recalled staring at Mary and Mathew.

'Then I noticed Mary and the boy, standing near the staffroom. They looked a little dazed and confused, so I guess I just plucked up the courage and went out to them, the whisky helping me of course.'

He then glanced at Mary, encouraging her to speak, so eager to take the spotlight off himself, as he had made such a mess of what he had said, painted an awful picture of himself, and he still felt so ashamed of his own selfishness. The lockers? How lame his excuse sounded for why he had gone through them.

And as for the reason he had plucked up the courage to go out to them ... well, it disgusted him. He was sure the others had their suspicions, labelling him as a fucking selfish coward. And after what he had said about his day, well, a childish, selfish coward...

5

MARY'S STORY

'My life sounds a little boring. Basically, I'm a full-time housewife and part-time student, and to sum my day up, it consists of looking after the two men in my life. What time I have left, I spend studying; I'm doing a course on bookkeeping, as I am hoping to work from home part time rather than go into full-time employment. It was Jamie's idea, said he would be able to attract a little business my way. Then again, I haven't actually ever been in full-time employment as regards working for an employer. But believe me, I am not shy of hard work, as I used to live and work on a farm. It was my mum and dad's.'

Mary wondered how her parents were, and she just hoped and prayed Spain hadn't been hit. She also hoped and prayed her brother Michael was okay. He lived alone down south, but then again he hardly ventured out and was a semi-recluse. He worked from home, some job on the Internet, had food delivered to the house and was extremely security conscious. She had often joked that if anything should happen to him it would take the police and fire service forever to get inside. And of course there was her cousin, who only lived two blocks from her. She had attempted to drive over there, but it seemed the neighbourhood was under siege with the crazed people, and the safest option had been to leave, which she did. The destination she had hoped to reach? The man she had been trying to reach? She imagined Jamie was with his colleagues, barricaded in the office, worrying to death about the two of them. He always worried about them, but recently had failed to show it. Then again, she was sure all men had a strange way of showing their affection, as if it was a weakness to show it.

She smiled as she recalled when she first met him. He had visited their farm, working for an insurance firm at the time and trying to sell them insurance. He was so handsome and was the sort of man she had dreamed of. He had visited them a few times after that, and she was sure it was more to see her than about insurance, as he would always make a fuss of her. She knew from then on that he was what she needed in her life, and that the world would be an interesting and exciting place to live in. She could see the same thoughts in Jamie's eyes and knew they were meant to be; that one-in-a-million chance of meeting the right one, the chemistry so right, chances definitely worth taking.

He had swept her away from the farm and brought her to the city. At first she was glad to see the back of the farm, to be free from the nest, free from the long, hard, boring days, but the city was not a pleasurable place to be.

The farm may have been a simple and boring life, but at least it wasn't a hectic and frustrating life like the city, expectations suffocating the advantages.

Since being in the city she had failed to find what she wanted to do, and had undertaken many night classes on different courses but without success. And the one she was currently doing was becoming difficult, and she was getting frustrated and bored with it, constantly seeking distractions.

She so needed to find something she would be able to do, as they needed the extra money. A chance for Jamie to work less hours, be at home a little more, and the chance for them both to sit and talk about each other's day, rather than it being one-sided.

She rubbed Mathew's head and said, 'Dad works too many long hours, doesn't he, sweetheart?'

She often thought when she was alone in the house, when she was feeling low, was this as good as it was going to get for them? Jamie living at work, hoping that by him doing so he would manage to dig them out of the financial pit they were up to their necks in.

But it had been so easy to fall into debt, what with loans and credit cards being offered on a plate. They needed to pay for their holidays, hobbies and other pursuits, the latest gadgets. Everybody quoted, 'You have to live for today! You only get one life, so live it! Life's not a rehearsal!' Yes, all destined for a pauper's grave.

So they had followed the advice, just like the masses. Dining out, chasing various leisure pursuits, the Corsa, the BMW, and her shopping habits, buying clothes, not forgetting turning their home into a palace.

Then the cost of living rose faster than an airship; pressure, constant pressure, so wanting to maintain the lifestyle they enjoyed, not wanting to cut back, even though the warning signs were there, shouting in the ear. Then finally the winter of discontent; not just them suffering, but the millions.

Is it any wonder what had happened had?

'My day had been one of leisure. I'd been down to the gym, and visited my cousin and we'd had dinner together. Then did a few chores I had been meaning to do, and as the evening drew closer, I prepared dinner, collected Mathew from school...'

She paused, recalling how boring her life sounded and felt deflated by it. Then she remembered what happened next, the horror that was to unfold, and finally said, 'I had left the dinner simmering in the kitchen, expecting Jamie home in about an hour, and Mathew was on his Xbox, so I sat with my coursework, reading what I had to do, trying to get my head around it all, as I had fallen behind. But then the lights went out, and moments later Mathew came running downstairs saying the electric had gone upstairs as well.

'At first I checked the fuse box, but it took me ages to get to it and when I finally did I noticed it hadn't tripped. I planned to call the electric board, but the phone line was down. And so was my mobile. At first I thought it must be a terrorist attack, but told myself no, I wasn't going to think along those lines, not put myself through scenarios. I had done that on the 7-7 attack, as Jamie was in the city then, and I had spent hours trying to get through to him, thinking he was hurt as he didn't answer his phone, when all along his battery was flat. And like back then, what was so frustrating was the fact that I didn't know what to do. However, I had a feeling, well, hoped that things would work again very soon, so until then we just sat on the sofa, and I told Mathew a story of old, expecting the lights to come back on at any moment. I mean, there had been one or two power cuts recently, but not one that affects communication.'

'The story mum told was a good one, a scary one,' Mathew added, his eyes lighting up at the memory; it had been a similar setting to the one they were in now, sitting in front of a candle. 'You should tell it to everybody here,' he said. Then he glanced at Ron and smiled. 'It will frighten you.'

'Another time, eh?' Mary said, kissing him on his crown.

'We then noticed how green the sky was, and just for a moment or two we stared at it, expecting something to happen. We weren't sure what was going to happen, but were certain of one thing: whatever did happen, it wasn't going to be good. I then grabbed my mobile to check if it was working, but it was still dead, and the landline too... It was then that I became frightened, and knew this was something really serious. It hadn't been like that even after the 7-7 incident. The thought of it being a terrorist attack returned, though this time they had obviously used something more sinister. I gave it another half an hour, constantly checking my mobile and the landline, but nothing... And all the time Mathew remained strong, positive,' she added, kissing him on his crown again.

Mathew blushed, though he had a huge smile on his face.

'So I decided we would visit our neighbours, see if they had heard anything; they were such logical, practical people, always seemed to have an answer for any problem or situation. Then again, they were ex-teachers, stable and strong.'

She recalled stepping out of the house and into a dreary haze. A diluted green haze, which seemed to sting the eyes. It resembled one of those bad B-movies, with an eerie scene setting that left you expecting somebody or something to jump out at you.

She had headed down the drive, Mathew by her side, and glanced up and down the street, intrigued to know what was happening. It was deserted, but then suddenly, about three hundred yards away, a man appeared on the street; he was kind of strange.

He had a look of uncertainty on his face, as if he was confused and yet menacing with it, as if rationality was clashing with irrationality, as if he was tripping on something terrible, something that was bringing the worst out of him. Then he began to run towards her, and then three other people joined him from nowhere, all destined for her. And the hate on their faces was so unnerving.

For a split second she just stared, knowing they were in danger, but too scared to act, the whole situation seeming so unreal.

She then recalled her neighbour, Mr Parker, coming out of his house, a dear sweet man in his sixties. The neighbour she had been going to see. He said there were strange people hanging around and told her to go back in the house, not to leave until the police had been.

But the strange people were running towards them and all she could do was continue to stare at them, curiosity and anxiety gripping her, not letting her do anything else. She was unable to listen to her trusted neighbour's logic like she had many a time.

What happened next seemed to happen so fast. The four strangers got closer and then ran straight at Mr Parker, attacking him like wild animals.

He screamed and screamed for help as they overpowered him, but all Mary could do was pull her son close, turn and run for the car, not wanting to see or hear, wanting to escape the horror. She longed to turn her back on it all, get her son to safety, away from what they were witnessing. And as she drove away, she recalled staring in the rear-view mirror at the angry mob who were now attacking Mrs Parker, tearing her apart as if she was a rag doll, her husband's lifeless body at her feet.

She recalled the feeling of relief when she escaped, but felt so awful for thinking like that, wondering if there was anything she could have done to help her neighbours.

'I decided to drive to my cousin's house, but the journey was to be aborted. Those crazed people were everywhere, nowhere seemed safe, so I decided to head for Jamie's work, hoping it would be safe there and he would be waiting. I tried the radio, but all I got was interference… The A1 wasn't too bad, but as we got closer and closer to the city centre the roads were gridlocked, the sound of car horns deafening. We managed to drive halfway down Camden Road before we came to a stop, and then I saw what was causing the hysteria … more violence. It was so unreal, so unjustifiable. And it was everywhere. People dragging other people out of cars and hacking and punching, gauging them; it was like one of those awful horror movies. It looked like a warzone, senseless.'

'I did intend to get out of there, but like the drivers in front of me I was also blocked from performing any manoeuvre by cars which had appeared behind me, although some drivers tried, the result catastrophic. So we had no choice but to chance it and travel on foot, and most of the other car drivers were doing the same. However, there were many arguing and fighting, some even using knives. Then there were muggings, children screaming ... it was just shocking, far too shocking. And for those people that had remained in their cars, some were being attacked, pulled out by the crazed and killed. As for our journey on foot, we travelled as fast as we could, trying to avoid being dragged to the ground, mugged or, even worse, murdered. And as we did so, I felt like crying, but knew that wouldn't help us...'

She recalled trying to shield Mathew as much as she could from what was happening around them, but it was so difficult, as there were men and women running past them and screaming, pushing and shoving, nobody having any time for anyone, flashes of butchery everywhere. People were falling over and being trampled to death by the masses, screams of help and anger clashing.

Terrifying screams as a woman was bitten and beaten by four other women down an alleyway.

Then there was a family being pulled out of a car, all trying to protect each other, but their final battle was for their own survival. Deafening sounds as guns were used, fires started. She then recalled seeing a shopkeeper aiming a gun at a man, telling him he would shoot if he approached, then filling the man with lead as he ignored his warnings. The shopkeeper crashed to his knees and sobbed, disgusted by what he had done.

And where were the police?
Overhead, filming.
Just filming!!
Big Brother Britain.
Fucking filming.
What good was filming?

'We just headed for King's Cross, desperate to reach Jamie, as I just didn't know what else to do, but the carnage was getting worse and I feared for our safety. I am sure Jamie would have gone mad if he knew the risk we had taken, even though it had kept us alive, and I was so desperate to try to reach safety of some sort, believing where he was would be safe.'

She paused for a moment, trying to digest the horror she had witnessed, but all she could see in her mind's eye was red, red and green, a horrible combination, and not forgetting the terrifying noise, the sound of so many emotions colliding, erupting in the atmosphere.

'I remember standing on the corner of York Way looking in the direction of the tube station, knowing he would just be one journey away, feeling for sure the trains wouldn't be running, but so desperate to get to him, so desperate to take the gamble. Then all of a sudden, two women came barging past us. I glanced in the direction they had come from and noticed more of those mad-looking people heading in our direction. I had the unfortunate experience of watching some of them attacking a bus full of people right in front of us and knew we were in mortal danger if we remained where we were. I then saw the two women heading into the Underground and realised how they had reached it with minimum fuss, so I decided we should follow, decided to take the gamble. I just hoped the Underground would still be operational.'

Mary glanced down at Mathew to see him wide eyed, remembering their journey; such a brave little man. She kissed him again and told him how much she loved him, not daring to look at the others, as she was sure they were all judging her, thinking her a horrible mother, risking her son's life just to reach an office block. She glanced at Emma, welcoming her to take the spotlight.

6

EMMA'S STORY

She smiled, out of pleasantness, though it was forced, as she didn't want to divulge a great deal about her life recently, the life the both of them had been leading, what they had been up to in the hours leading up to what had happened. No, she never liked talking to people, it felt so alienating to do so, apart from the obvious ones, but they were only after one thing. However, these people were different, the sort to pass comment or judgment, which was why she hadn't said a great deal so far and didn't want to, especially since they had been in the company of a police officer. She had learned quite a while ago not to say too much in front of them. She believed they judged you by the way you looked and the people you were in the company of; she had seen it endless times. And the policeman they had been unfortunate to have to spend an evening with had failed to convince her he was any different to the rest. During their short spell with him, especially the previous evening, he hadn't once taken his eyes off them, probing them with his eyes all evening. And as the evening had turned to night, not once had he fallen asleep, as if he was afraid to in case they robbed him. Yes, he had failed to convince her otherwise, merely strengthening her beliefs.

And they were supposed to represent honesty and integrity, treat everybody the same, and yet it seemed to her that they were nothing but fascists, only interested in promotion and making other people's lives a misery, at whatever cost. Hounding the likes of Jake and her was easy promotion material; pick on the weak.

As for the rest of the group, she sensed they had begun to judge, condemn without saying anything, looking upon them as idle street scum because of the way they looked and dressed.

But who were they to judge them?

There was the woman with the child, who had obviously risked his life for the sake of reaching her husband, instead of making the child's safety her priority, exposing him to the madness and chaos on the streets, letting the boy witness murder and rape. What sort of mother and person did that make her? Irresponsible and selfish? Emma felt sure that her husband was with his fancy woman, possibly even hoping she had died so he could start again. She just knew the way the male species worked, especially the ones with egos; she had taken plenty of money from them.

Then there was the tube worker, an obvious alcoholic, possibly the reason his wife left him; yes, taking the worst drug of them all. Then there were the flaws in his character, never one for responsibility or pride. As regards his daughter, it seemed as if she wanted very little to do with him, and she obviously wasn't working and running with a bad crowd, so he had no reason to judge her, and she couldn't blame her daughter, as Emma would disown the likes of him.

And finally, there was the wounded woman. She had obviously fled and left people for dead; it seemed to

Emma that she was just a selfish bitch who had obviously got what she deserved.

None of them were perfect, probably far from it.

All destined to get what they deserved. So they all had no right to judge.

No right at all.

And as regards her life, what was there to say?

What did they want to hear?

To sum it up, it had been a life of wasted opportunities.

Is that what they wanted to hear? Did they want to know how she was practically in the gutter when it happened, just one step above those crazed things?

Give them something to gloat about, to lighten up their miserable existence. Is this what it was all about, just to find out who the biggest loser was?

Society, so stinking.

And what had she been up to in the last twenty-four hours? Soliciting, stealing, anything to get through another fucked-up day. Is that what they wanted to hear?

And yes, before they judged her as a waster, she could have done anything with her life. She had the wealthy parents behind her, both in high-paid jobs. Had a good education, did well at school and college, could have and should have gone on to university. She probably had more qualifications than all the people she was sharing the room with; a better pedigree than them.

That was one thing *she* could gloat about.

And as regards university, she had been planning to train as a nurse, or perhaps a social worker. Something cool, something that would make people look up to her. But the decision to go to uni wasn't to be rushed; she was sick of studying and hearing her parents praising her, and just needed a little time away from it all, to let off a little steam. She felt as if there was something missing in her life, a hunger that needed feeding, so she had decided on a year out, to attend as many wild parties as she could, live a little and enjoy life to its fullest. You know, while she was still young. Feed the hunger to live; perhaps that was what she so needed.

And as for the year out, her parents would bankroll it, just as long as she went to uni once the year was up; this she had promised.

Then she met Jake, at someone's birthday bash.

She recalled how wicked, good looking and dangerous he was. He warmed her soul, ignited a fire within that almost dissolved her melancholy way. It thrilled her to be with him, and the longer she was with him the less appealing university became, the less appealing a career became and the more she liked what he fed her – his habit.

She simply wanted to turn her back on the world and be with Jake, with or without her parents' permission.

It was a tough price to pay.

She remembered what they were doing before the explosion. She had been with a client less than an hour before; the indignity of a fifty-plus-year-old man on top of her, having to breathe in his odour, stale alcohol and BO, trying her best to turn off, let him have his pleasure, then away he would be.

And away he did go, hurrying back to his wife.

Jake was waiting for her outside the hotel, a grin on his face, eager to get his hands on his share of the money, not once asking if she was alright.

They had planned on heading for the Underground, to pickpocket one or two people during the late-evening rush hour, the elderly easy prey, but first they headed for their hideout. They had actually gone there to hide their money and have a little pick-me-up, what she so needed after being with that man. And that's where they were when the explosion happened. She recalled hearing noises, hysteria, and they had stared at each other for a while, wondering what on earth was happening, both waiting a while, letting the hysteria calm a little, waiting until things were a little quieter before venturing out. They noticed the city was in darkness, people rushing around everywhere, screaming and yelling, but they went in the direction of the Underground, near where they were, knowing if there was shit going down, pickpocketing would be so easy. She then recalled hearing one or two people shouting something about terrorists, others going on about murder happening everywhere.

On reaching the Underground, they noticed it was so dark down there and seemed deserted, though there were one or two people lying around, motionless. Emma had checked to see if they were okay, but they weren't, they were stone dead. Jake went through their pockets, stealing their wallets, and then suddenly the policeman appeared.

Jake claimed he was just looking for their identity, and put down the wallets.

But she did not want to tell the others this, as they would never understand.

Never understand.

Nobody understood.

Nobody would ever understand.

Her parents never could, so how could she expect them to?

'There's not a great deal to say,' she said, feeling a little pressured in to saying something after being silent for a while. 'We were just around Islington when it happened,' she said, not wanting to say any more.

She glanced at Lisa, welcoming her to say whatever she wanted, but she had seen the way they all looked at each other, the scepticism in their eyes, a look she had seen many times.

All wondering what she was trying to hide.

A look she had expected.

A look she had become used to.

7

LISA'S STORY

'First of all, excuse me if I pause, as I am still in a little pain. Anyway, my sister Vicky and I worked for a small printing company on Hungerford Road. Only seven of us work there; design brochures and pamphlets. We was due to finish work at three but stayed on, as the boss was away and wanted us to, and we did need the overtime since we were going to Paris in a few weeks' time; we'd been planning a girls' weekend away for quite a while. You know, going on the Euro train, first class, staying in a four-star hotel in the city centre; guess you could say we were going to do it in style. And to be honest, I had a bombshell to drop on them, but I was to tell my sister and family sooner, possibly over dinner. Then I'd tell the others on the train.'

She tried a smile, the thought of what she had to tell her family and friends warming her inside. She had been planning for weeks how she was going to do it and had even imagined the sort of reaction she would get, and that thought had kept her buzzing, knowing it would make the weekend even more exciting.

'I mean our other halves have done it enough when it comes to partying, always having their weekends away.

So it was a chance for the girls to let their hair down, have our share of fun, which we hadn't done for quite a while. Our last chance together before things started to change.'

She smiled faintly, realising she was in a room full of strangers, possibly going to share the secret with them before her precious sister, who would never get to know what she had to say. The thought sent her cold, so she chose to say nothing more on the subject, the pain of not telling her sister so strong. She realised that even if they did all get out of the situation they were in alive, the weekend would never happen, she would probably never go away ever again, so there was no point in talking about it.

How could she do anything again, knowing she left her sister to die on that escalator in the hands of those murderous bastards? Yes, left alone in the dark, dying. No, she didn't deserve to go out, didn't deserve a life. She only deserved what she was destined for, a life of pain.

She then had a flashback to being on the escalator, her sister just in front of her, screaming, begging for help. The darkness as terrifying as her screams, the whole situation becoming so unbearable. She recalled trembling and crying, not sure what to do, everything so unreal and frightening. Then she remembered racing towards her sister, but instead of stopping to try and save her, she just pushed past those hurting her sister, slipping on the steps and tumbling to the platform, before getting to her feet, totally blinded by the darkness, and fleeing.

What a crime.

What a fucking crime.

Then there were the two work colleagues they had left to die.

'There were two other people with us in the office, Jimmy and Caroline...

Jimmy was a robust character, larger than life, and he had a way of lighting up a room when he entered it...'

And as she spoke, visions of the recently deceased entered her mind, all laughing and joking the way they always did. Then Caroline's sharp tone entered her mind, not liking too much fun, and yet Jimmy always mocking her and eventually having her in stitches.

'The demand for what we were producing had gone crazy, and we were struggling to keep up. Some of our clients were so fussy, but then we had Jimmy as head of creation, Caroline head of editing, so bound to please and at the same time the pair of them bound to clash. We sure had a lot of laughs with them. We had nicknamed Jimmy "Christopher Biggins", and he would boast how he would teach him a thing or two. Well, Jimmy had been making us laugh for most of the day, keeping up morale, as we were practically having to live at work. Work being a chore, sure can be tedious. And as I stated before, the reason we were doing the extra hours was self-inflicted. Every last one of us guilty... Then again, money does buy luxuries, and had bought far too many for me on the plastic; even most of the holiday had been paid for on the plastic.'

She smiled, even though she was in pain. Constant evidence of the pain was on her face in the form of sweat, but memories of Jimmy made her smile, would always make her smile, as he never seemed to let anything get him down. Always had a smile and a joke to tell, just knew how to pick people up when they were down, always quoting, 'A day without laughter is a day wasted.' She recalled many a time when she had been out shopping with her sister and they had bumped into Jimmy on Oxford Street. He would be weighed down with bags of shopping, dressed flamboyantly with a long pretty silk scarf around his neck, face flustered, and yet his eyes lighting up at their presence, eyes that were made to look bigger by the glasses he wore. And within a second he would have them both laughing, telling them about some pickle he had found himself in, expressing the scenario with hand gestures and rolling his eyes to add a little drama, always finishing his anecdotes by stating how he hadn't let the situation get to him.

'Jimmy sure was a great laugh, always raised a smile, especially when we had some form of function. Yes, always liked being the centre of attention. And even when the explosion happened he made a joke of it.'

She recalled how the joke was a little weak by his standards; had nobody laughing.

'But being honest, his joke was a little hollow, as for the first time in my life, since I had known him, he looked scared, especially when the lights and everything else went down. At first we just sat there, expecting something to happen, but not sure what, definitely not another explosion. When it had happened, we were all so terrified, lost for words, not sure what to do, trying to get our mobiles to work, trying desperately to contact loved ones, find out what had happened... All of us were far too terrified to leave that room, and therefore we sat for quite a while in silence, all of us preoccupied with our thoughts... I guess Vicki, like myself, was expecting my Wayne to come and rescue us, but no, nothing, then a little while longer. Jimmy started rambling on about how he wished there was a hunk in the room, just trying his best to make some banter; then he was silenced as the banging on the door started.'

BANG! BANG! BANG!

Lisa shuddered as she recalled it.

BANG! BANG! BANG!

'It was loud and frantic, and believe me, none of us dared to answer it, even though we knew it could be somebody seeking help.'

BANG! BANG! BANG!

'We all had that gut feeling that there was trouble, serious trouble. And the banging continued, it just wouldn't go away. Then moments later, Jimmy made a joke about it, said he couldn't believe that people were desperate to get in, when most people wanted to get out. We all looked at each other, wondering what to do. Was it somebody seeking help, or the police? We just weren't sure, but the frantic nature of it told us something just wasn't right.

'However, it was Jimmy who answered the door, and I'm sure deep down he didn't want to, but he did the masculine thing, even though, believe me, I was probably more masculine than he was. He even tried to make a joke as he went to open it. Shouted first, though, asking who was there, but there was no reply, just more banging.'

BANG! BANG! BANG!

She paused and her eyes clouded, the pain of what happened then so unreal; the beginning of the end, tragedy striking so sudden and so fast, her life unravelling in minutes, plummeting into darkness at a blinding speed, from having everything to live for to having nothing to live for.

'And when he did open the door, it just seemed to happen so fast.'

She recalled seeing Jimmy being overpowered by half a dozen people, all soaked in something, all looking wild. Jimmy screamed as they pushed him backwards.

'They pinned Jimmy to one of the desks while they tore the flesh from his body with jagged instruments, and all Jimmy did was gargle blood, roll his eyes, reach out with his hands, seeking help. I was terrified by what we were witnessing and couldn't move. Just could not move... It was Caroline who went to help him, but they turned on her and just overpowered her as quickly as they had overpowered Jimmy.'

Lisa recalled Vicky gripping her arm and telling her to run, to keep running.

But before they did, she had looked down at Jimmy, who lay on the floor, blood seeping from him, a faint glint of life in his eyes, feeling pity, helpless.

She then recalled them leaving the room, leaving the building, with Caroline begging them to help her and not to leave, neither of them daring to look back, to see what her fate and theirs would be if they remained.

'My sister and I ran in to the street, and for a moment or two all we could do was stand and stare at the horror that was before us. Everywhere we looked there were people murdering other people, cars out of control, plunging into buildings. Other cars running into people and some engulfed in flames, people staggering out of cars engulfed in flames. Then there were looters and muggings, people, young and old, running for their lives, and as for the noise, it was a collision of screaming, shouting, crying, just unbelievable, so unbelievable and so terrifying. Law and order had diminished and it was a free for all, society on meltdown.

'Vicky started running and I just followed, and everywhere we went it was the same carnage. During our desperate flight, not once did we speak; we just fled and cried, wondering what was happening and what was going to happen to us. I guess like my sister I just wanted to run straight in to the law, but they were nowhere, just nowhere.' She smiled faintly. 'The police are never around when you need them.'

She then continued in a serious tone, the pain of what happened next so painful.

So real.

'We headed for the Underground, as we had some of these mad people chasing us. They seemed to have targeted us as we headed onto York Way. I guess we were hoping by doing so we would lose them. On reaching the Underground I stopped for a moment so I could get my breath, my younger sister being fitter than me. But Vicky just continued to run. I shouted for her to stop, but she didn't listen, just continued to run. Just wouldn't listen, she wouldn't listen. So I began to run again, trying to catch up with her, but I wasn't sure where she was planning on heading. I just followed, plunging deeper into darkness, straight into the tunnels and down the escalator. I never once looked back, just carried on going…'

She paused and wiped tears from her eyes, the horror unfolding in her mind, unravelling her logical mind; so much horror, madness and confusion, far too much for her to handle.

'Then those crazed people grabbed Vicky; they seemed to have been waiting.'

Her voice broke and she wanted to cry again. She recalled Vicky screaming for help, but her screams terrified her, and it was so dark, so confusing and so unreal.

'They grabbed my own sister, and all I could think of doing was running, and to keep on running. I left her to be butchered by those crazed things.'

She paused for a moment, wiping the tears that flowed, reflecting on the strong bond she had had with her sister, a twenty-six-year bond, but how quickly it had shattered in a moment of despair. Haunted by her sister's glowing eyes, her laughter, haunted by the good times, times she would never see again, and that very thought aged her. She then glanced at the others, noticing they had their heads down, as if they knew something. Perhaps they were wondering how could she have left her to die like that.

'I ran down the tracks and continued to run, and believe me, I wanted to stop, so wanted to stop, as my lungs felt like they were bursting. Then eventually, I reached this platform and at first I just did not know what to do but cry. I made my way up the escalator, realising I had been hurt really bad. When I had fallen down the other escalator, I must have landed on something, as there was quite a lot of blood, and by then I was struggling and needed to sit down. It was then that I noticed the office door was open, and I sat down where you found me and cried, and did I cry.'

She began to cry, trying to get her head around why she had left her sister to die.

Why had she?

Then she thought of the others and imagined they must be horrified by her selfishness, all thinking she had deserved what had happened to her and perhaps deserved to die.

Yes, she deserved to die.

8

Day 2

EUSTON UNDERGROUND

2.32 p.m.

They all went quiet, reflecting on what they had said, feeling vulnerable and exposed. And if that wasn't enough pain, they felt physically numb and cold, nauseous and restless. Mental and physical exhaustion was not too far away, and they were left wondering, once it was all over, where their lives would go from there.

In Lisa's case, she wondered how on earth she was going to pick up the pieces of her shattered life, and had been wondering since she found herself in that office. And yet she had always viewed herself as a strong person, able to cope with whatever life might throw at her, Vicki often saying how she wished she was as mentally strong as her. Many a friend thanking her for always being there for them in times of crisis. She was known as the iron lady, and she imagined her friends were all saying how they wished they had her with them, yet she so wished she had them with her.

As for Mary, she had been reliving so many memories she wished she could forget, but she knew they would haunt her for the rest of her life, memories of the masses she had witnessed being murdered, from her caring neighbours to people she did not know, savaged by human animals, showing no mercy or purpose for their onslaught. As a matter of fact, everyone in the room had witnessed slaughter and she was sure, just like her, the whole situation was breaking their hearts.

She then wondered how John and Jake had got on.

Had they run into more survivors?

Or possibly help?

Or just maybe into...

She didn't want to consider the worst.

No, she had to be optimistic.

Had to be, as there was nothing else left in their lives but hope, their darkest hour upon them.

Ron recalled his dead friend, imagined how he had fought many of those things, holding them off as long as he could while folk fled. He deserved a medal for his bravery, so deserved a medal, and when it was all over Ron was going to round up what friends were left and have a damned good toast to Barry. He considered what he wanted right there and then, what he needed: a cigarette and glass of whisky. Yes, he could do with that toast now, something to numb the anxiety and pain, and how he kicked himself for leaving his whisky behind.

As they sat waiting and thinking, the minutes seemed like hours. Emma so needed a fix and was getting frustrated, wanting Jake to hurry back. Then a little while later came the knock they had been waiting for, hoping and praying for. All smiling, they got to their feet, eager to know how they had got on.

John was the first to enter, looking flustered and a little stressed. He stepped aside so Jake could enter and as he did so he immediately hugged Emma, both whispering, then telling the others they needed to slip out to use the toilets.

Then finally, an elderly couple entered.

They introduced themselves as Keith and Margaret, shaking everybody's hands as if they were old acquaintances, sounding a little cheery, glad to be in their company.

'Welcome,' Ron said, being the last to shake their hands. Then he glanced at John, waiting for an explanation, some good news.

'We made our way along the tracks, which was an awful journey, possibly worse than the journey we had to get to here ... so we will definitely have to head for the surface to continue. However, back to our journey... We came to a train, which was stationary in the next station. That's where we found Keith and Margaret.'

John suddenly had flashbacks, recalled seeing the rear of the train, all of its lights out, daunting and unwelcoming. He had scanned the platform as they got close, his heart going crazy, adrenal glands on overtime, noticing it had been really bad, with a dozen or more dead, mutilated bodies, then the alarming sound of banging coming from within the train. And at first John wasn't going to head in to the train, and intended heading straight for the surface, but no, his policing got the better of him. He had considered that if there were crazed upon the train they might be trying to get to survivors, or perhaps they were just trapped in a carriage, but either way, he had to know.

'Did you get any hassle, you know, did you meet any of those things?' Ron asked, breaking into his thoughts.

John nodded, recalling creeping through the train, gun ready. Then it all happened so fast, in a blur. The crazed man seemed to come from nowhere, but hit the floor with two shots imbedded in him.

'Just the one was on the train.' He glanced in the direction of Mathew, who was listening, and he chose his words carefully. 'We dealt with the situation. Then a moment or two later, we met these two.'

'What is your next plan?' Keith asked in his cheery voice, turning to face their saviour.

'We wait until it gets darker and then head for the surface, find some transport. We saw nothing worth taking on the return journey. Then we get the hell out of here,' John said. He glanced at Ron and added, 'But first, how about we have a cigarette out there, before we shut ourselves in?'

Ron agreed, eager for a cigarette. Jake and Emma returned, looking uplifted.

And while they smoked, Ron explained to John, Jake and Emma how they had introduced themselves, and how they had got to where they were. It helped to shed light on things.

Then he asked if John wanted to join in, which he did, and they returned to the room, feeling a little lifted after their much-needed cigarette. Ron, Mary and Lisa explained their stories again, trying to not get too bogged down emotionally as they had before, keeping it brief. When Lisa had finished, she glanced at John, welcoming him to begin, all eager to hear the policeman's story, all eager to know what the law had to say for itself, all so annoyed and feeling cheated with the so-called law. As for John, he felt so alone.

9

JOHN'S STORY

'I had been sitting with some of my colleagues in the canteen, listening to old Bill. Old Bill being the sergeant, used to be in the army and boy, did we know it. He was going on and on about the recession and how he had predicted it. Saying how surprised he was it had taken so long to materialise, moaning and groaning about prices and how they had risen even more since the start of the recession, how it was affecting people, folk looking depressed, stressed, and some extremely aggravated, looking for someone to take their frustrations out on, and most of the time how that was us, simply because we were on the front line, the punchbags for society, when they should be taking it out on the politicians. He said the politicians had a lot in common with the captain of the Titanic, said they had seen it coming but were so ignorant of the danger, too busy trying to impress. Then he went on to say that those police who would keep their jobs would possibly end up being some of the few that would benefit from the recession, with an increase in break-ins, robbery, violence and so on. There was bound to be overtime for us, possibly by the bucketload, and old Bill hated the extra hours, basically hated most things. Then he quoted again how he was going to ask for his pay-off if there were to be redundancies at the station. And I know old Bill was a bore, but being honest, we would sooner have been sitting where we were, listening to him groaning, than be on the streets, especially after the weekend we'd had.'

He considered the weekend, dealing with drunks, fights and domestic problems. It seemed that when the weekend came and darkness descended, people's energy level rose to breaking point. All fuelled by the three demons: alcohol, drugs and money. There were a hell of a lot of Dr Jekylls and Mr Hydes about. Then, come daybreak, they couldn't apologise enough, claiming they didn't know what had come over them.

But John knew, just as he had stated before. Too much alcohol, too many drugs and not enough money, bound to create problems, bound to create frustration. And these problems were happening everywhere, people just ticking away, like a time bomb.

Then bang!!!

'All weekends for the Met are barmy, believe me, and just recently, every day seems a hassle. Anyway, back to old Bill... After his rant and when he had finally run out of steam and made a temporary exit, basically to refill his coffee cup, the rest of us began talking about what we had planned for the coming weekend, our weekend off, wanting to talk about something positive, lift our mood.'

John's weekend was to be spent with his girlfriend, Debbie.

He then drifted in his thoughts, trying to understand where their so-called relationship was going, just like he had done many a time, as it seemed to him that they had reached a stalemate, unable to go in the direction he wanted it to, and it had been that way for months.

Then again, from the beginning she had made it clear to him that she wasn't after any serious commitment, wanted to take things steady, but he had wanted to see her more and more, as being around her brought out the best in him, but Debbie wanted to focus her energy on promotion at the bank. As time passed, he believed there was a strong connection there, believed she was a little nervous when it came to commitment, using the bank as an excuse to shy away, believed they were soulmates. He just needed to convince Debbie that, and he had tried.

He would often text her, though sometimes would never get a reply, which had frustrated him. Often he would drop everything when she called and wanted to see him, and that would frustrate him even more.

When would she realise how much he really felt for her and how far he would be prepared to go for her? He had told her often enough.

But he wasn't with her then. He had run and hid rather than trying harder to reach her, the situation becoming a little too much for him.

He wondered if the disaster would be a blessing in disguise, as she was probably barricaded in the bank that she loved so much, wishing she was with him, knowing the building she was trapped in wasn't going to make her happy. Maybe she would realise it would only trap her, like it was doing right now. She would be wanting and waiting and hoping he would rescue her.

Rescue her?

But he did try to reach her.

How he had tried.

But there had been no through route to the bank, every route in the Strand being chaos. He would never have reached it without finding himself in serious trouble. That was why he had run and hid, to get his head together, because he was falling apart, shell-shocked by all he had seen.

'Then the explosion… There were officers running around the station, rumours circulating. We were told it had happened somewhere near Central London, affecting the electricity source, plunging most of London into darkness. We immediately thought that terrorists had struck. But we didn't have time to consider it, as old Bill was barking out his orders, drafting us immediately into a van. He told us to wear our chemical warfare outfits, told us it was serious. And as we boarded the van, I noticed the sky was a green colour.'

He reflected on the terror and uncertainty he had felt, wondering how Debbie was, wishing he could call her, but duty came first.

Just like Debbie.

And he was regretting not texting her when it happened, when his mobile was working, before the second explosion.

'All the training we had had regarding a chemical attack was supposed to prepare us for what we were expecting, but you could have heard a pin drop in the van, and as we headed to where the incident was, we were redirected. Told we had to head for Downing Street, said we were being deployed as riot police and not for front-line chemical warfare support, told to keep our outfits on though.'

He paused as he remembered staring into one of his colleague's eyes who was sat opposite him, the same colleague he had been laughing and joking with less than ten minutes before the incident.

He had been going on about his wife and children, telling John not to get married or have children as they were hell, saying how John had got it right, and yet John was sure he could see regret in his colleague's eyes, wishing he was with them right then, with the people that really mattered in his life, just like the rest of them.

'On the approach to Downing Street it was bedlam; we could hear shouts, screams and explosions. The van was bouncing and rocking, and we knew we were going over debris, so were sure it was really bad, and the Strand wasn't too far away, so Debbie was on my mind again. Then finally, the van came to a stop in Whitehall, the doors opened and as we got out we saw two or three hundred other police officers dressed like us, all standing around, awaiting orders, armed with riot shields and batons, backed up with tear gas, water cannons, and there were helicopters in the sky, buzzing around like flies. And yet the other officers looked as baffled as we were… Though what was so terrifying was that we could hear screams and cries swirling in the wind and coming from nearby, heartbreaking it was. And while we stood around we heard various stories circulating of what had happened, of what we were to expect. Officers were going on about civil unrest, a mob heading for Downing Street, most of the politicians being flown out of the Commons and Downing Street, Whitehall being evacuated, foreign delegates also being evacuated by helicopter, destination all hush-hush. And behind the gates of Downing Street there were armed special forces, and rumours of an emergency meeting underway.

'Suddenly, a whistle went and a PA system was activated, giving our group leaders orders, where we were to be deployed. Basically sealing off Whitehall, Parliament Street and Richmond Terrace, told who we were expecting could come from any direction. Told we were there to bolster the Whitehall police station's ranks. So we waited… We could hear screams and explosions coming from afar, the thundering sound of horses as there was a police charge under way… Then all of a sudden they came; there must have been two or three hundred of them, running like hell down Parliament Street. The police lines beyond there had failed…'

John paused, reliving the roar they had made as they surged forward, sending an icy chill down his spine. And the might of that roar told him and his colleagues that they were in for one hell of a fight.

The only way they would be able to stop them was with guns.

'Faster and faster, so eager to get to us, so eager to crush us, and as they got closer we caught a glimpse of their faces; they looked as if they were high on something, and whatever it was had driven them mad. I mean, their eyes were bloodshot, and foam was coming from their mouths. Believe me, we were bricking it behind those shields, had our heads buried, clinging on to those shields as if our lives depended on it. Yet old Bill kept barking out his orders. "Don't break the line, boys." And as for the water cannons and tear gas, they failed to break their stride. They just ran on and on, destination us. Then impact!! They hit us with such force, it was as if we had been hit by a car.'

John paused again, recalling the moment of impact, the shudder they felt, some of his colleagues hitting the floor, looking dazed and confused. Then their loud cries again and the sound of the helicopters beating above, the helicopters that were just filming, just damned filming.

And old Bill shouting, shouting.

'The line broke within seconds ... and I just remember looking around, feeling a little dazed and kind of isolated. I could see police officers on the ground, being attacked by these people ... and they showed no mercy, just gauging and biting. It was awful, and yet I felt there was nothing I could do, I felt helpless. I heard an officer shout, "Watch out, more on the way, coming from the Embankment." Apparently they were surrounding Westminster, and there were also rumours that some of the officers had gone crazy, attacking other officers.

'Then hell broke loose as officers used guns ... and yet it failed to deter them. They just overpowered the officers using them. Police officers then began dropping their shields and running, running for their lives ... stripping off their protective gear, ridding themselves of the handicap of the uniform and running. I mean, what chance do you have against God knows how many of these crazed people, who would not stop until you or they were dead?'

'I remember glancing at a colleague of mine, on the floor. Three of them were on top of him, biting and hacking away... He had reached out with his hand, begging me to grab it and try to free him from the suffering, but all I could think of doing was running, dropping my shield and running. Stripping the gear I wore and running. Getting away from there as fast as I could, and what convinced me to definitely go through with it was when I heard the special forces start using their guns; they didn't care who they shot. So flee I did.

All I was bothered about was saving myself, my fucking self, just like so many others. And all you could hear was people crying out for help and the sound of those helicopters.'

He recalled running through the streets, passing mothers with children being attacked, all crying for help, wanting his help. Pensioners being pulled to the ground and hacked to death, but like everyone else, he just ran. And the faster he moved, the more it became a blur.

He had desperately wanted to reach Debbie, and had even tried using his mobile, but the phone was still dead, fucking stone dead.

'It was sheer hysteria, everyone screaming and fighting, cars crashing into each other, people crashing through shop windows, looters running off with their gains. And as for the swirl of noise, I never want to hear that ever again. I have never felt so petrified in my life and I was supposed to protect people, be there for people in times like that, and yet I was as frightened as them...'

'I then came across an armed police officer. He was standing in Leicester Square, next to a statue, yelling at a group of people, warning them he would shoot if they approached him. The people looked confused, wanting protection. I paused and studied the officer ... he had this dazed look about him, his clothes torn and shoddy, and when he looked at me I could see the sorrow in his eyes... He then pointed the gun at his head and pulled the trigger.'

He recalled wiping the blood and brains from the man's face, taking the gun. The man's hand was still warm, still a weak pulse, and he was gargling and grunting, foamed saliva and blood coming from his mouth. He remembered the scooter he stole while the rider was trying to give a dying woman first aid. He just wanted to reach Debbie, so wanted to reach her, at whatever cost.

He then headed for the Strand, but there was no through route as everywhere was the same, just murder, fucking murder, mobs killing, looting and desecrating. He recalled a woman engulfed in flames. She ran towards a shop, inside which was a family, along with the owners. The owners sealed the door, not wanting her to enter. Then a car hit the woman and lost control, with the burning woman on the bonnet, and it ploughed straight through the shop window, exploding moments later. The noise of all those people screaming and crying for help was too much for him to handle. Then he headed for Islington, the police station he was based at, but wondered what on earth he was going to say. On reaching Islington, it seemed the violence had spread, and he felt so broken, disheartened, so he dumped the scooter and wandered in to the Underground. It just seemed the right thing to do, to escape everything.

'I eventually made my way down here, to try and get my head together... I thought about the dozens and dozens of people who had cried out for my help, and I had turned my back on them. I felt like crying, I felt so hopeless.'

He glanced at Jake and Emma.

'And while I was wrestling with my conscience, I spotted Jake and Emma. They said they knew the Underground a little, so I stayed with them. We spent the night in the gents' toilets, then this morning we intended to hit the surface, but it was still really bad, bodies everywhere and those things roaming. So we decided on the tracks.'

He thought about when he had met Jake and Emma. They had looked a little pissed off when he approached them, as if they didn't know whether to run or stay. He knew then they were stealing from the dead, not the sort to be trusted or liked, and he didn't sleep that night. No, he could not take his eyes off those bastards.

He glanced around the office, seeing them staring at him, and asked himself what he would do if the worst came to the worst and they were overwhelmed by those things again.

Would he run and leave the others?

Then again, why should he care what happened to them? He just wanted to reach Debbie.

And he was sure that after what he had divulged, their opinion of him would be one of low admiration, and perhaps he had been too graphic. He was sure Mary and her son were horrified by him.

He glanced at Jake, encouraging him to take the spotlight.

He was intrigued to know what he had to say, though deep down he imagined most of it would be lies or distorting the truth. His sort were all the same – not to be trusted.

10

JAKE'S STORY

Jake kissed Emma on her forehead, told her how proud he was of her, how much he loved her. Told her whatever he said he meant and that he would always be proud of her. He had no shame in anything they had ever done, as it had kept them alive, they'd done it for survival. He believed you always had to put yourself first when it came to survival, which was why they had survived. As for those who thought they were better than them, well, most were dead, so they were not as great as they thought. What was the point of being clever when all you really needed to be was canny?

He held on to her hand, knowing she had probably said very little, always timid when it came to talking about their life. He turned to face the others and began.

'We have, as you have probably guessed, been sleeping rough for a while now, but being too proud to ask for help, too proud to beg on our hands and knees like the millions and live on state handouts; it's been tough getting by, and I know it's partly been my fault. I have been on a downward spiral for years, getting involved with drugs and everything else that goes along with them, and I am not proud of it, believe me, I am not proud at all, as they take over your life and destroy everything that is worth anything... Then again, I have always taken them to ease the pain of my life. Yes, it's been tough. I spent my young days from twelve onwards in various hostels, until a few years ago when I finally got myself a flat, and then eventually met Emma. And she means the world to me. She's turned my life around, given meaning to it.'

He squeezed her hand, letting her know he appreciated her, as words weren't his strongest point, and they would often fail him when it came to letting her know how he felt, how much he appreciated her support and devotion.

'I thought my life was turning around, but drugs have always been a love and hate relationship for me. I guess my love and dependency on them was so strong, as they would always pick me up when my self-esteem was at an all-time low, and that would be often when I had taken them, as I felt so low for taking them, so dirty and disgusting. Yeah, just a vicious circle, I know. Then you try finding a job in this city when you have no qualifications and a history of being in trouble with the police ... and like I mentioned, a low self-esteem, and believe me, I have tried to find work, but somebody will always kick you in the teeth when you are down... And boy, have I been down ... so down.'

He recalled his painful adolescent years, the years that hurt so much. His parents splitting up when he was young, him being left with a drunken mother who beat him until he was taken in to custody.

He then thought about his fiery teenager years, not so long ago, only three years; they had been a waste. Ran with some extremely bad boys, the hostel boys, boys that had nothing and wanted everything, at whatever price, and he was addicted to the hard stuff back then. Therefore, in the process he had done some extremely terrible things, which was why he ended up in prison.

And as for prison, he thought it was tough, so tough, and what really annoyed him was the idiots who have never had a day in prison, quoting how soft they are, how lenient.

Twenty-four hours of boredom and frustration, a hell of a lot of moody and bullish people to contend with, having to share dorms with murderers and rapists; he was so sure those sorts of people really don't have any idea. And while he was in there, he recalled there were three suicides. That's how easy prison was.

He had often thought, if it was that easy, why don't they give it a go?

And who wants to know the likes of him when he had been to prison?

He then remembered how hurt he was when he first met Emma's parents. It had taken a lot of courage to go and meet them, and he recalled waiting outside in the rain, waiting to be introduced to them, smoking about three or four cigarettes. And on being introduced, how they had judged him as a wrong one; he had seen it in their eyes, their mannerisms.

'Well, Emma moved in with me and we eventually got thrown out of our flat, landlord saying he didn't want undesirables living there.' He laughed, which was forced, and then said, 'It was a right dump anyway, and hey, you wouldn't even entice cockroaches to live there, that's what a shithole it was. Then on leaving we tried staying in hostels, but those places were full of lowlifes, wanting to rob you of anything they can…

And they brought back so many bad memories for me. Also there's the fear of bumping into some of your old so-called pals. So we chose the streets. And when you are on the streets you take drugs more,' Jake said, leaving out the colourful, regretful detail that came with a life of drugs and decline, surviving on the streets at whatever cost.

The look in the policeman's eyes annoyed him, and he imagined he was judging them for all the wrong reasons, not wanting to try to understand them, just wanting them off the streets, wanting them behind bars, out of sight and out of mind.

Society stinking.

So stinking.

Jake then became aware of how horrified the others looked; the look he had seen most of his life. Just like the policeman, thinking they were better than them because they worked and paid their way, doing their bit for society. As for Jake and Emma, it was a case of being told to get a job, told they were the lowest of the low. Everybody wanting to cast their negative energy on them, blame the likes of them for their wrongdoings. Like it was Jake's and Emma's fault they couldn't meet their mortgage payments and so on, and yet it wasn't the likes of Jake and Emma who had created the recession or the situation they were in. No, as far as he was concerned it was the likes of the people Jake and Emma were sharing the room with that had created the problems; they had a lot to answer for.

'And when it happened we just headed for the Underground, you know, to take shelter, as it was mental everywhere, and while we were down here we saw some guys lying near the ticket machines and checked if they were alright, you know, doing the decent thing,' he said, not making eye contact with anyone.

Jake then recalled them being down there, going through that man's wallet; there must have been near on five hundred pounds in there. Then the excitement built within, the task of pickpocketing made so easy, just there for the taking. But their dreams and gains were dashed by the appearance of John. He just seemed to appear from nowhere, and boy, had Jake wished he would go back to nowhere. That evening, in the toilets, while the policeman stayed awake all night, Jake had pretended to sleep, just lying there with his eyes shut, occasionally peeping to see if the policeman was asleep. If he had been, they would have slipped out of the room and disappeared, but not before taking those wallets. But no, that wasn't to be, the fucking policeman was like a prison guard. It seemed that no authorities trusted them; all bastards.

He noticed how they all continued to listen with their heads bowed, trying to hide their disgust. But who were they to judge him? Because after what they had said, they were more criminal than he would ever be. With the policeman deserting everyone, looking out for himself, just like all police, and no doubt he would slip away and desert them all at some stage. Then there was the pissed-up tube worker with an obvious alcohol dependency, failing to do his job, well, practically failing at everything in life. Then the woman who had risked her kid's life just to reach a man who was probably dead like the endless God knows how many others. Then the woman with the bad leg who had left her own sister to die, but who was seeking their pity.

As far as he was concerned, every one of them was as guilty as sin when it came to being sinful.

He couldn't wait to hear what dark secrets the elderly couple had; no doubt there were plenty. Jake was sure they had done nothing to be ashamed of, just had to do it for survival.

Jake offered them all his chocolate bars, which they accepted. It seemed they were more than happy to except his gains, so what did that make them?

In Jake's eyes, hypocritical, cynical and human.

Yes, human.

He then glanced at the elderly couple and smiled, intrigued to hear their sins.

11

KEITH AND MARGARET'S STORY

'We had been out for most of the day, taking it extremely easy, doing a little window shopping around King's Cross and Euston Road. Then we found ourselves on Regents Park. We had taken a picnic with us, and though it had been cold we still loved dining outdoors, kind of romantic,' Keith said, a warming smile upon his face as memories returned of their little picnic.

'We never would have imagined in our wildest dreams this was going to happen … never.'

He paused, face serious as he reflected on the nightmare that had unfolded before them, flashbacks of what happened in the tube station returning thick and fast.

Then he said, 'We were just looking forward to getting home and relaxing, having a bath and chilling. We had been to our own little shop on Warren Street just before we decided to head off home, collected a few items out there, as we sell new-age clothing, holistic supplies and natural cosmetics, though business is a little slack at the moment and I'm sure we don't need to explain why. Well, back to the incident… We boarded the tube train at Warren Street, and like always it was so packed, though a young couple offered us a seat, bless them, and before the train moved there was a tremor that shook the train. Moments later the lights on the platform went out and the train made a slight droning sound, though it was still not moving. For a moment or two everybody remained silent, though all observant, apart from the odd person muttering, like always on the tube. Then within a flash everybody in the carriage started to panic, and there was some man going on about terrorist attacks again.'

He recalled the man's words. He was shrieking something about an explosion nearby, people dying, ranting on about terrorists. That was when the hysteria set in, fellow passengers all getting to their feet and joining those already standing and rushing for the doors, forcing them open and leaving, without their belongings.

As for Keith, he had just held onto Margaret's hand, hoping they were overreacting.

Praying they were overreacting.

He recalled an elderly woman who sat opposite them, who had often glanced in their direction, wondering what the best course of action was, before finally getting to her feet and following the other passengers.

'The comments from that man caused the hysteria. Some of the passengers then forced the doors open, screaming and shouting, and then fled, just leaving belongings and almost trampling on fellow passengers... Anxiety sure brings out the worst in people... Shocking, just shocking.'

Keith gripped Margaret's hand, just like he had before.

'I told Margaret that whatever happened, I would be right by her side, and I advised her it might be best to remain on the train, as it could just be some kind of power cut. And we had seen our share of hysteria in our time, having been on many demonstrations, so we knew how crazy people can get over the slightest thing... But when the second shudder happened and people began screaming outside of the train, it dawned on us that this was serious. I then asked Margaret what she wanted to do.'

Keith glanced at Margaret, allowing her to take over.

'I was quite happy to remain where we were. I believed there would be a solution to it at any moment, well, I was hoping there would be,' Margaret said, recalling how petrified she had felt.

Even though they had been on many demonstrations in their lives, seen crazy many times, it was still frightening, and they believed demonstrations of recent times were all violence, which was why they had stopped doing them. And this was just terrifying, had something extremely sinister about it, and for possibly the first time in their lives they prayed the police would show up, wanting the brute force of the law.

She glanced at Keith, welcoming him to take over, not really wanting to talk about the violence.

'But then the hysteria got worse, as people were practically colliding into each other on the platform, trying desperately to escape something... We got to our feet and stared out of the window, to try and understand what was causing all the bother, expecting a bunch of unruly beer-drinking thugs to be approaching, but that wasn't the case, no, not at all... There was a large group of crazed-looking people. I mean, they just looked like your average person off the street, dressed in suits or casual, some young, some old, just so much diversity, and yet they were all attacking people like wild animals, as if they were on some kind of drug. I mean, they looked wild and crazed, and were seriously harming people,' Keith said, tears welling up in his eyes as he relived the madness in his mind. He felt the terror he had felt back then, and was reliving the shrieks of people as they were attacked, seeing a hand hit one of the windows of the train, smeared in blood.

He remembered making an attempt to head for the door, but wasn't sure why. Probably to escape, help or run like the rest, but he was stopped by Margaret.

'I decided it would be in our interests if we moved from the carriage we were in, as the door had been forced open and there were some of those mad people nearby. And luckily for us, there was still some battery life in the doors and the lights, though they had dimmed. So we settled in another carriage, where we remained until John and Jake arrived.'

They shared a faint smile, recalling how harrowing it had been, sitting there, hearing those people outside banging and yelling, but without words. Yet the noise they made was terrifying, wanting to get in at them, wanting to harm them, but why? And it was the not knowing why that frightened them. It had seemed like a lifetime in that carriage, as if they wouldn't be rescued and might even die in there. Yes, their thoughts were harrowing, but neither spoke, they just clung onto each other's hand, listening to their own heartbeats.

Then all went quiet for a while, and finally, they heard the sound of a gun as John and Jake arrived.

They had never liked guns, always protested against them, but they were glad to hear the sound of this one.

They greeted their saviours with joy, hugs and the odd kiss, so overjoyed and expecting that to be the end of it all.

But no, that was only the beginning. Next came the daunting and terrifying journey to where they were now, but they had gained a little comfort in the thing they detested – the gun.

On the surface, the carnage, death and destruction was an upsetting sight, so upsetting, with no sign of help, and on two occasions they had to hide while some of those crazy-looking people appeared, as if they were seeking them, hunting them down.

Both felt an overwhelming sense of relief to be sitting where they were now, back in the land of the living, feeling that the dreadful nightmare was now coming to an end; well, at least they hoped it was.

As for Keith, he couldn't help but wonder what had happened to the elderly lady. He wished he had said what was on his mind when she looked in their direction, looking for someone to advise her on the best course of action. Keith would have reassured her, told her to remain where she was, and he was sure she would have.

So sure she would have.

12

Day 2

EUSTON TUBE STATION

3.17 p.m.

The moment Keith and Margaret finished their story they all went silent, reflecting on how lucky they were to have made it as far as they had, visions of the many close encounters with those things going through their minds.

They felt so much remorse for those that had been attacked, those that now lay dead. They all started thinking about what now mattered, what was important to them, their loved ones on their mind, all hoping and praying they were fine, not daring to consider if the worst had happened to them. They had been there already, and knew how tiring those thoughts were. They thought about the many people they knew and had met in their lives, praying they were also fine. Visions flashed through their minds of the many happy times they had had with those that mattered, sunny days returning thick and fast. Days spent basking in the sun, talking about what they wanted to do, what they intended to do, nothing but idle talk, but great talk, uplifting talk. They vowed that if they got out of this situation alive, they would do something they had promised to do but had always put off doing. Turn yesteryears idle chat into reality.

They thought about those irritating little things that had been grinding them down, such as people's annoying habits, worrying about using too much electric, just everyday worries and cares, which now seemed meaningless, yet they all wished they had those problems rather than those they had now.

One thing was for sure, though, when this nightmare was over, and if they were lucky enough to survive, they would make the most of their lives and put what regrets they may have behind them. And as regards the little things that bothered them, they would just shrug them off and move forward. At least then they would have gained something positive from the situation, even though it was just a very small step forward step; yes, something positive from something so negative.

They all found themselves drawn heavily into thoughts of their loved ones, with feelings of desperation to get to them. They each found their own corner of the room to try to reorganise the syntax of their lives, and to lick their wounds.

13

JOHN

John thought about his parents, the first time since the incident. No, not once had they entered his mind, though he had over the years trained his mind to block out thoughts of them, not wanting to spend his energy worrying about their welfare, as he was certain they wouldn't consider him. However, there was a time when he had had endless sleepless nights back when he first fell out with them and walked away. How he had longed back then for them to call him, to attempt to contact him, but they had disowned him the moment he joined the Met – the beginning of the end.

His dad vowed he would never speak to a son who joined the forces. Said the police were government lackeys, challenging them during the mining strikes, thinking themselves superior to everybody else. "How could anyone want to join that filth?" he had said, telling John he had to choose between his family and the force, as both would never work.

Then again, his dad would say many things, as he always had an opinion on most subjects in life, criticising everything and anything, never happy unless he was complaining about something, making a stand against something or someone. He lived a life of frustration, well, that was how John viewed it anyway, wanting to make everybody's life as miserable as his. John was convinced his dad was a bully and so he was glad to be away from him, as far away as possible, out of sight, out of mind.

And as for his mum…

John had always felt for her, and could never understand why she stood by their so-called father. Putting up with endless insults and being classed as inferior. Even when John walked out, his mum had stood by her husband, just like his brother when it came to choosing between accepting what her son wished to do or her wicked husband's beliefs, having neither a voice nor a mind, always tiptoeing around him.

It seemed his mum enjoyed playing the perfect little housewife, going around boasting about how long they had been together, nearly thirty-five years of marriage, the talk of the north, but at what price? As for his brother, the perfect son, well, he was just a waster like his dad, with no intention of working, just going around with some hard-faced fascist bastards who all obviously had a chip on their shoulders with everybody and everything. He was a bully like their dad; dad's ideal son. Both mother and brother just lackeys of a bitter man, both best forgotten. All three best forgotten.

None of them had ever tried to contact him, and if it hadn't been for his bike and a handful of trustworthy friends whom he had gone through police training with, he may never have survived. So they had become his family, his adopted family. All there to support him and chase away the blues whenever they came knocking. And he was worried about them, but deep down, so deep down, he was worried about his own family more, even though he was trying his best not to admit it. How he hated himself for doing so; he thought he had conquered his feelings towards them. He was sure, though, that deep within their hearts his family would be worried about him too, especially his mum.

He then wondered about the person that really did matter, Debbie.

Wondered if she had managed to escape from the bank.

The bank she adored.

And if she hadn't and was still in the bank, had she been telling everyone about how John would rescue them, raising their hopes, only to feel disappointed when he didn't make it, her head bowing as time slipped away?

Her work colleague, Fiona, would be quoting how he was like all men, a total let-down. A total shit. Hadn't got the nerve to push on when it mattered.

Perhaps Debbie was questioning how he felt towards her.

Shit! he thought, recalling something important, something extremely important. Something he hated himself for not remembering.

She always finished early on a Monday, and would spend the whole evening in her apartment, her wind-down time, watching something on DVD with a glass of wine. She shared the apartment with her colleague Fiona, who would also stay in on a Monday, and they would have a takeaway. God, what an idiot he had been. He was sure he deserved all the slagging off Fiona would be delivering.

He then focused his thoughts for a brief moment on Fiona. Her very name made his muscles tense. Debbie and her were practically inseparable. Worked together, lived together, played together.

Fiona drove a flashy car and spent a mint on cosmetics, clothing and whatever else went with her image.

She was superior to Debbie at the bank and would often fill her with big ideas. Always bragging how great it was to be a singleton, fancying herself as one of the women from the TV series Sex in the City. She had a string of lovers, one of whom would meet up with her two or three times a week. She was always boasting how she had him eating out of her hands, saying how men were the weaker sex.

He wondered if she was so brash and flowing with confidence right now. How big had she felt when she saw what was going down? He was sure most people like her crumbled under pressure, and he imagined Lisa was a lot like her, as she had fallen apart when it came to make or break time.

But would Fiona crumble?

And if she had, would she be irrational just like Lisa?

Would she have advised the pair of them to do something erratic, and possibly endanger their lives?

Hopefully she would have kept her head together, had the sense to advise Debbie to barricade themselves in the apartment, as it seemed Debbie would follow her to the ends of the earth. And if they had barricaded themselves in, perhaps they had done so with one or two of their neighbours.

The neighbours were mostly flashy singletons, Fiona's sort of people; wine, cocktails and caviar, and whatever else goes with their so-called image.

When Debbie and Fiona were together they were like a double act, so no doubt if they had neighbours with them they would be keeping their spirits up with their endless wit and charm, possibly even throwing a cocktail party, making the best out of a bad situation. If it was to be the end of the world, at least go out with a bang. And Fiona was no doubt using her mentally positive attitude to try to gain something positive from it all, always seeking something positive in everything they did, always having the last say in everything.

He recalled the many times Fiona was with him and Debbie, and he had felt a little intimidated by them, left in the cold, and just had to sit and listen to Fiona banging on. If he chose to make some input, he would have to be careful what he said to stop Fiona commenting or passing judgment, as she so often would. She had a razor-sharp tongue and loved using it against him, loved mocking his northern accent, especially in front of their neighbours.

John thought about their neighbours again.

There was a couple living on one side, a casual relationship they called it; basically a pair of ageing swingers, embarrassing in his eyes, the sort of people who probably go on those sex dating sites, seeking as many sexual diseases as possible. And then there was a bachelor living on the other side, quite well off, having made his money in property.

John had often seen the way Debbie looked at him whenever they were leaving her apartment and he was either leaving or entering his. She would go out of her way to say hello, make him laugh, make conversation, their eyes lingering on each other.

Then she would continue talking about him, commenting on something he had bought or a holiday he was booking. She seemed a little breathless, looked a little flustered, her eyes wide, the extravagant and bashful lifestyle of her neighbour touching her heart.

How could John compete?

Many times he had hoped and prayed he was a closet homosexual. But what was eating him up was the thought that Debbie might be keeping it casual with him while waiting for this bloke to show an interest in her. Then it would be farewell to John, and he was sure Fiona would advise her to do just that. Yes, Fiona was sinister.

And what had set the alarm bells ringing was that if they were barricaded in the flat together and did have feelings for each other, would they be admitting them?

No doubt Fiona would be reminding her of what a let-down John was.

No doubt her neighbour would then look even more tempting.

John suddenly found himself wishing her so-called neighbour had been murdered by those things. If that was the case, would Debbie then want commitment from John on seeing him again, the crisis reminding her how precious life was?

He had passed jewellery shops many a time, browsing at the prices, considering which one he would purchase when she wanted to take their relationship in the direction he wanted it to go. He knew it sounded pathetic, but that had been the reason he had been doing the overtime, so he could buy her the best.

Fuck it, he had thought.

Fuck it!!

He would ask her when he saw her again, find out if there was going to be more to them than sex now and again, more than just a weekend away and the odd date here and there.

And if there wasn't going to be anything in it, then fuck it, it would be over; greener pastures bound.

Greener pastures ahead.

He then wondered what tired him the most, the situation they were in now or his plaguing thoughts of Debbie...

14

RON

Ron tried to consider what his daughter would have decided to do regarding her safety. He had been trying since the crisis to think through the possible scenarios, believing her to be wise enough to look out for herself. She was not the sort of person to become irrational; no, far from it. She was more like him, burying her head in the sand, finding a place to hide until the panic calmed a little, and then find someone rational to stick around with. Yes, that would be the wise thing to do. But the creeping doubt kept haunting him of whether she would be wise enough to do that. Would she? She had become attached to that bunch of lowlifes she lived with, and if they panicked, would she? They definitely didn't look like the type to consider a rational plan, to hide until the crisis passed. No, they would probably be looting, and that meant his Libby could be too, and how risky would that be with all the crazy people about? Boy, did he so hope he was wrong.

As regards his Libby's motives and actions, he had been trying to figure them out for the majority of her adult life. Basically it seemed as if her life was as messed up as his own, hanging around with a bunch of dropouts just like he had done most of his life.

He recalled again the last time he had seen her, less than twenty-four hours ago, when he had dropped by to give her fifty pounds so she could spend it on her mobile and a little shopping she wanted to do. He had thought how thin she looked, and ended up giving her sixty pounds and told her like he always did to get something to eat.

He was sure she could do with the extra money, because apart from what she received from unemployment benefit, Ron was her only other source of money. But at least he still looked out for her, not like her mother, who had just turned her back on her, given up on her own flesh and blood. What sort of person could do that apart from a cold, callous one? Then again, that was the sort of person she was, callous. It had taken Ron an awfully long time to discover that; the warning signs had been there, but ignored, until bang. That had been years ago, yet it was as painful as if it happened an hour ago. Ron had had to find out the hard way what a sinister bitch she was, and they hadn't spoken since. Thoughts of her still stung him, angered him. He wondered if she was still alive. Had she survived with her lover boy, now husband?

He was sure if she had, she would be hoping he hadn't. She would have loved him to die, longed for him to die, probably hoped her daughter had died as well, to wipe out all traces of the old family she wished to forget; that was the sort of woman she was.

She had used Ron, cheated on him, and he had been the one to walk away with nothing. He had lost everything, just because her fancy man could afford a flashy lawyer, one that ruined him, made out Ron had made no effort in the marriage. His fault that the relationship had collapsed, never being at home, always at football or out on the bike. He would often spend time in one of the many drinking holes, wasting hours rather than being at home with his family, spending his time doing anything rather than supporting his family. He was also the reason behind their daughter's decline in society. He was blamed for everything and labelled a failure. But her solicitor had failed to mention that she had been spending hours at work, sleeping with her boss and God knows who else in order to get a promotion.

Now who was in the wrong?

Then again, he was doomed from the beginning when it came to the divorce, since it was a female magistrate. Bastards all stick together.

Well, who was the one who had been looking out for their daughter recently? Yes, it was him.

Even though he wasn't there for her during her adolescent years and early teens, she hadn't been there either, leaving a child minder to bring Libby up, and what a failure she had been, but he made up for it now.

And as regards his ex-wife, he had heard rumours a while ago that she had claimed it was his fault their daughter was a tearaway, taking after him and destined to be a loser like him. Yes, she still had a venomous tongue.

That was her excuse for washing her hands of her. Perhaps she had been poisoned by that fucking husband of hers, the man who had impregnated his wife and given her twin daughters. They were her life now and all that mattered to her, both growing up politically correct, destined to be part of society's snobbery, the society that was wrong with the country.

Well, Ron's Libby was all that mattered to him, and it would kill him if he never saw her again.

He had to find her, had to. Just had to know she was fine.

And he would not rest until he managed that. Somehow he had to get to her apartment, being the obvious first place to check up on her, just in case she was there, waiting for her dad, just like the Libby of old. And just like the dad of old he had been drinking, shirking his responsibilities when he may have had a chance to reach her. The old Ron returning to haunt him, the man he was ashamed of.

15

MARY

Mary considered what Jamie and her would have been doing right then if what had happened hadn't.

She had no doubt she would have been at home, expecting Jamie to enter the house with his work colleagues and business clients at any chosen moment. He had planned to finish work early that day; he would only finish early when clients were involved. And while she waited she would have been checking over the spread, making sure she hadn't forgotten anything, making sure the wine was room temperature and so on. She would have been flapping around if she had forgotten something, and more than likely she would have done, as there was so much to consider, so much to do, so much to remember, everything having to be right. Otherwise, a possible failure and Jamie would always be the first to point out something that wasn't right, and she didn't like letting him down, so enjoyed seeing him happy, even though at times it had made her miserable.

She would then try calling Jamie to delay their guests, knowing he was entertaining them down the road at a chosen establishment, just a five-minute walk away.

That would then give her enough time to travel to the supermarket, cursing herself for forgetting whatever she had forgotten, and no doubt while heading to the supermarket she would be answering text messages from Mathew, who would have been planning to stay at his mate's house, just like he always did whenever they had guests, before getting home with minutes to spare, the final preparations being finished as they approached the house.

She would then greet them with a smile, take their jackets, with Jamie helping her, standing side by side, being as welcoming as possible, Jamie then making a fuss of them again.

Yes, she would be acting the perfect wife-cum-servant. She would fill his colleagues' glasses with wine and make sure there was plenty of food, dashing here and there while listening to their laughter and jokes, knowing then it was a success, another success.

And as the function matured and the guests mellowed, business being pushed to the back of their minds, she would then find the guests asking questions such as, how was Mathew, how well the house looked and what alterations were they planning next, where were they going to spend their next holiday, and when they were going to trade in their cars for newer models, some of them boasting about what they had bought or intended to buy. And of course the banter flowed as freely as the wine, and one or two of the guests would jokingly ask Jamie if he had a bit on the side, as he was away from home for such a long time, teasing him, just like they always did. Jamie would just blush, kiss Mary's hand and state she was all that mattered to him.

And the more she reflected on it, and this not being the first time she had, it seemed that Mary wasn't all that mattered to him, not as much as his work. Their life, their lifestyle, their family, all revolved around Jamie's work. And if ever she raised her concerns, he would always remind her how they needed the money.

Money?

But what good was that when they were in a situation like the one they were in right now?

If it wasn't for the money and his ambition, Jamie would have been home the previous evening, instead of them being separated, Mary left wondering if he was alright.

And what would he have been doing the previous evening, the evening when it happened?

She was sure he would have been sat in his office, working on deals and plans, possibly even working on his final preparations for the following day, for the function. He had turned into a different person since his promotion just under a year ago, wanting to go further, slowly but surely marrying his job.

Yes, impressing his employer, like a dedicated soldier, well, that's what his boss called him; one hundred per cent workaholic, and what was always frustrating was the fact that he would never answer his phone whenever she called him, and she would always have to leave a message, wait for him to get back to her. His job came before her, before his family.

And as regards the incident, she knew whatever had happened it had been really bad where Jamie worked. She only hoped he was barricaded safely in his office, wishing he was with her, possibly telling all his colleagues about how it was all going to change when it was over, how his marriage was going to come first, to hell with work... Well, she hoped, so hoped, and she was sure that if she could get to his office and he witnessed their arrival, he would realise how much they thought of him; a kind of wake-up call.

Perhaps then they could sell their house, downsize, get a cheaper mortgage; they could also sell one of the cars, cut right back, get rid of their debt so they could spend more time together, be a proper family, and maybe she could just get a simple part-time job rather than trying to be ambitious.

They could even visit their parents more, instead of calling them every now and then, and Jamie's family as well. She smiled to herself. She would love to do that, and so longed to change things.

She found herself feeling sick with worry for them, for everybody she loved and cared for.

She dwelled on what had happened and what she had witnessed, and hoped those who had survived like they had would all reconsider what really mattered.

She thought perhaps it would be a wake-up call for Britain, or even the entire planet, time to focus on what mattered, placing the value of family and friendship over everything else, because the love for money and power had so far failed to deliver anything but evil. No, money doesn't buy happiness.

All that mattered to Mary right then was getting to Jamie, and she wouldn't be able to rest until she knew he was okay, because that was why she was where she was, suffering like the others, just to reach him.

Yes, Jamie was her destination.

16

JAKE

Jake stared at Emma, noticing how depressed she looked. She had been looking that way for a while now, long before the incident. He recalled the life they had been living, both relying on the money she made and what pockets they could steal from, most of the time from the elderly, those they could rob and flee from quickly, never once considering they could be caught and both be facing a lengthy prison sentence. They needed fast money, their lifestyle demanded it, and so they just ploughed on ahead, to hell with the consequences. Even though they had to live with what they were doing, he was sure of one thing – he would never have made it without Emma, and may have resorted to worse. He would have more than likely been a hell of a lot more reckless and been back in prison way back, or dead.

So their relationship had saved him. She had saved him, made every wrong turn seem like a right one. It was all worth it, just as long as he had Emma.

He then considered their relationship.

From the beginning it had been a blur. They had met on a night out and had text each other before meeting again. When they had, it was to be on another night out, both getting wasted before meeting up. It had been that way for the first week or two, only meeting once pissed. And Jake was sure back then she carried a lot of hurt and frustration like he did, and was sure the reason she was always drunk like him was to mask that pain.

He remembered Emma telling him about her parents, who, as far as he was concerned, were out of touch with reality when it came to the young and their desires, especially Emma's desires, wanting to push her into doing this and that, banging on about how the future was more important than the present, no idea of the importance of living while still young.

Her parents were typical middle-class shits, expecting her to do well. Any sign of Emma enjoying herself was, in their eyes, a definite step onto the slippery slope, and he was that slippery slope, the fucking distraction to ruin, the one she could definitely do without.

Jake recalled meeting her parents.

A failure, that was what he was to them, judged by the way he looked and spoke.

And that hurt, it hurt like hell.

He knew deep down he wasn't the only failure, as they had failed to see the hurt and frustration in Emma, failed to see what she needed rather than what they wanted of her.

He guessed that made them a bigger failure than him, and perhaps they had sensed that, and that was why they hated him so much.

Every time he went round they'd start asking him questions, wanting to know more and more about him.

Digging, digging and fucking digging, seeking the dirt they needed to hate him even more.

What had he done in the past for a living?

Had he ever held down a full-time job?
What were his interests?
When was he planning to get on the property ladder?
Question after fucking question.

As for interests, he didn't have any; they were just a boring waste of time and effort. And as for the property ladder, what was the point?

Working all hours right up until you were practically too knackered and ready for the scrap heap before the house was paid off.

And in current times, working to pay off negative equity.

Pointless.

All fucking pointless.

Then, as time went on, they would be whispering as he entered the house, whispering as he left, commenting on how untidy he was, always picking fault, never happy, so determined to drive a wedge between him and Emma. No, they wouldn't be happy until her heart had been broken, and they were responsible for breaking her heart again. The only way they felt they could mend her heart was by throwing money at her, buying her, though ironically they both came to rely on that money.

He then recalled the day Emma came round to his flat with all her belongings, saying how she had rowed with her parents and this time she had decided enough was enough, ranting on about the things that had been said, harsh words flowing freely, destination pain.

Then she started to go on about how she wanted to move in with him, and at that present time in their relationship she was only staying with him at weekends. Wow, how crazy the weekends were; two nights of solid drink and drugs, followed by wild sex. And her parents would sub her the money. Sub their weekend parties.

Yes, the money?

The money they had bought her with, the money they both needed. The moment she had walked out of their lives, she had also walked away from that money.

One hundred and fifty pounds a week was an awful lot of money.

Food and bills would drain what dole money he was getting back then.

No money then for drugs or drink?

No more wild weekends?

He would rather go without food than drugs and drink, but when he had done that before, he had made himself extremely ill.

So money was needed.

Easy money needed.

Then the idea of prostitution came to him while they were having sex, as she would often want to role-play, and liked him to act as different people, liked him to be a little rough and sometimes kinky.

Although at first she seemed a little unsure, went a little quiet and withdrawn, she did eventually warm to the idea. Jake had to nudge her in the right direction though, filling her head full of big ideas. Yes, she liked to hear his big ideas and boy, they could earn more than the handouts her parents gave her, a hell of a lot more. Therefore, there would be more drugs and drink to get them through the fucked-up world.

It was then that he gave her her first taste of heroin. He knew she needed it as much as he needed to get back on it, the last time being before he went to prison. He had been a prisoner to it, and he knew she would do anything for that hit. There would be no chance of her getting cold feet then.

She would walk the streets while he sat by the toilets watching, seeing the smile on her face, the sparkle in her eye as she talked to a punter. Then she would get in the car, Jake wondering every time if one of the punters would sweep her off her feet and steal her away from him, leaving him sitting there in the cold, alone, and that thought terrified him. Yet not once did he think she might get hurt.

He even found it hard to have sex with her, wondering if she had had a bigger knob inside her, one that made her wish she could have it regularly.

And what really put him off sex was the thought of what was going through her mind while she was sleeping with the punters.

When she had returned from a client, she would be so full of herself, fanning herself with the money she had made, boasting about a tip she had had, thinking herself as the prostitute out of Pretty Woman.

And yet he welcomed the money.

So welcomed the money.

The thought of going back to that life when this was all over just didn't seem appealing at all. She had started to keep regular clients, keeping their identity private, not letting him know anything, taking the prostitution a little too seriously. Then again, perhaps she was after a way out of their relationship, hoping one of her clients would sweep her away. Therefore, it had to stop; there had to be a way of capitalising on the situation they were in, a way of getting money fast. There had to be.

He then considered what he had many a time since leaving the shop with the chocolate and cigarettes. It would have been so easy to steal from the till, so easy. He had to find a way to make lots of money, and fast.

There had to be a way.

Had to be…

17

EMMA

Emma glanced at Jake, noticing how relaxed he was, as if he couldn't give a shit about anything. Then she thought about what he had said as regards their drugs and lifestyle. He'd told them everything she didn't want to, and she was sure they were thinking she wanted to hide it, because no doubt now they would be thinking the worst; doesn't everyone? Thinking they weren't to be trusted, not to turn their backs on them, expecting them to rob them if they had the chance, and as for the policeman, no doubt he was feeling he had been right not to take his eyes off them, proud of his judgment. No, they were not to be trusted. It seemed trust had to be earned, and you had to have merit to be trusted, like the so-called policeman; it seemed everybody was trusting him. And as far as Emma was concerned, he was probably looking for an excuse to get away from them all, as he seemed a little agitated and lost in thoughts of places he'd rather be.

And as regards the word trust...

That was something Emma had failed to see in people a long time ago. Far too many people had exploited her, exploited both of them. Then again, was there another way to learn?

She then wondered again why he had told them.

Why tell complete strangers of the awful way they had to live?

Why?

Was it out of ego or guilt?

She then wondered if he was aware of how it hurt her whenever he divulged anything regarding their lives; he did have a habit of telling people and they would all smirk.

Was he aware how upset she was about the way they lived?

It was as if he thought his dangerous image would impress, when all it did in her eyes was show the world how they had failed, how easily they had given up on life, given up on the fight to achieve dreams, and what had they settled for instead? Apart from what Jake bragged about, they were living in a derelict house they had broken into, with no running water or electric, and the only time she showered was at a client's hotel room or house, having to do the laundry at a laundrette, sleeping on a mattress on the floor.

She had often cursed the day she had tried heroin, as she had never wanted to get too involved with drugs, had intended to use them for social purposes only, just at weekends, like so many other young people. But no, not for her, not any more; she needed them, and needed them every day. It was an addiction she had failed to admit to until now. An addiction that had drained all the goodness from her, leaving her just craving for them, and to hell with how they got them. But she hated living like that, hated the way they went about feeding their habit, and the very thought of going back to that life when the situation they were in had passed was upsetting. Yet she felt so hopeless, so weak towards that life, as if she was in chains to drugs. She needed a fix very soon and was sure Jake did too, so she hoped he had something on him stronger than what he had given her earlier.

The ugliness of their situation hurt like hell and she didn't need reminding; never mind telling strangers.

Why hadn't he kept his mouth shut? she wondered. *Why doesn't he ever keep his mouth shut? Whenever he opens his mouth, it just gets us into trouble.*

She had given up everything for him: her parents, the chance of going to university and most importantly her self-respect, sleeping with men just to raise money for them, to feed their disgusting habit. She had even kept her clients a secret to protect him, and had even pretended to enjoy it just to please him.

And when had he last made love to her, shown her affection, made her feel special?

When?

Did he realise how depressed she was?

No, he wouldn't, because he was always wrapped up in his own world, focused on self-destruction, too fucked with the world.

She had often wondered how long it would be until he started telling everybody in his casual way about how she raised most of their money. That's if he hadn't already done so.

No, he wouldn't, she thought. *He would never do that.*

She considered what had drawn her to him in the first place. She had questioned it many times recently, and she remembered when she first met him.

At that birthday bash she had felt so out of it, so alone, only invited to make the numbers up. She had stood on her own for most of the evening, and then Jake just appeared at her side. He had the most amazing smile and magnetising eyes, and made small talk with her. He cheered her up, made her feel so wanted and special, and they sat in the garden and she told him about the frustration she was feeling, with her having wealthy and extremely opinionated parents who had expectations of her, and that because of them, people she knew despised her. Jake had listened to her and made her laugh, helped her to forget all that was bothering her, all that annoyed her, her parents. The parents who would always be hell-bent on making life difficult for anyone who tried to get close to her, and those that did, they would always drive them away; they had managed to do so before.

They wanted her to be boring and plain, and had even dressed her that way as a child. How she hated it, being plain Jane, and she resented them for doing that to her.

Her life had seemed flat and pretty empty until she met Jake. Him entering her life had detonated an explosion of feelings she had longed to feel, all surfacing at the same time. There had only ever been a few other boys that had done that to her, but they had been quickly driven away, but not Jake.

Yes, Jake was a wild card, but he was a breath of fresh air in her life, and the only man who remained by her side even though her parents tried their hardest to drive him away.

She had respected him for that.

Jake was quite a character, his philosophy in life being 'expect nothing from anyone, then never be disappointed'.

He was so welcome in her life, so needed; different and dangerous.

But where had his philosophy got them?

And where was it destined to take them?

Prison maybe?

And it wouldn't be for a short time for Jake, for either of them.

She then recalled her mum saying she was just a phone call away if she should want to go home, but *he* must be off the scene.

No, mum wouldn't be happy until plain Jane was back under her thumb again, being treated like a doll, put on show when friends visited, just like before. Not allowed to talk, mum doing all the talking, saying what her daughter was going to do and so on, then no doubt packed off to university. Out of sight, out of mind. Ringing once a week just to check up on her, possibly even turning up at uni to make sure there was nobody else on the scene.

Perhaps the situation they were in now would make her parents want to get in touch with her.

Families wanted to be close when there was a disaster.

Then again, maybe she should call them when it was all over.

Perhaps they were praying for her to call.

In the back of her mind, something that had been bothering her for quite some time resurfaced, a nagging doubt, that just maybe her parents were right about Jake.

What had been her dad's words, the words that had made her walk?

"He's nothing but a bloody leech, scum of the earth, a useless piece of filth. Just like the rest you have been out with."

But Jake hadn't said anything to the others to convince them he was any different.

Perhaps she would be better off without him.

Perhaps her parents did know best.

She realised she had some serious decisions to make, some extremely serious ones. And perhaps she would gain something out of the incident; maybe it would shake her into making a decision, a decision that was long overdue.

A decision she had to make.

18

KEITH

Keith glanced at Margaret and smiled. Since they had been in the room, Margaret had tried her best to keep morale up. They still had bits and bobs in the picnic basket, which she handed out. Mathew was grateful for the sausages and crisps, and Ron and Mary thanked her for the sandwich; the others declined, but thanked her for the offer. It seemed to Keith that she just had a natural way of bringing out the best in people, and how he adored that about her, realising, like so many times before, how lucky he was to have such a wonderful woman for his wife.

He reached in his pocket and grasped his chakra charm, silently thanking it for their luck at having escaped the horror they had witnessed. All that mattered to them was each other, not like the poor people they were sharing the room with, all so eager to be with someone, or the people they had shared the train carriage with, all so anxious, so desperate and eager to reach their loved ones, having to put their own lives in danger to do so, and some having lost their lives in the process. He was so lucky his loved one was beside him and had not had to make such a sacrifice; all they had to do was follow the others to safety.

He reflected on how fortunate he had been in life to have someone he so loved by his side for over forty years, someone who understood everything about him. He silently reminded himself of it most days, and had often told her how lucky he was, but not as much as he would have liked to. She truly was the reason he felt so alive, and if he ever felt down, she would pick him up, have him laughing in no time, using her Margaret Magic, as he called it. Yes, he had something so special and precious, someone who made the darkest of days seem like a walk in the park.

If there was something worrying him, she would talk things through with him and then finish by reminding him that as long as he had his health and they had each other, that was all that mattered, as worries come and go. They always pass. She would say moods were like the weather; they change. Like situations and incidents, they pass. You just have to be strong, stay sure and focused, and then even the toughest of situations can be overcome.

And boy, had they had their share of situations, their share of confrontations with police, governments and others come their way. They had been true socialists, both committed and caring people, believing in people before power, people's people; yes, true socialists.

He was sure the government and other heads of states were behind the incident they were up against now, and he knew the government would pay; there was no way they were going to sweep this one aside. There would be serious questions asked, answers wanted.

It seemed to Keith that all the government wanted to do was spread bad karma, create friction, create class divide, therefore socially dividing people, creating splinter groups that thrived on bettering themselves at any cost, profits and stature more important than human emotions. And no doubt those sorts of people had bought their way out of the current situation, but why should Keith care any more? It seemed nobody else did, and the thought deflated him.

Keith thought back to the tube station, the horror that had unfolded, the memories so graphic. He still felt numb and shocked by what they had seen, and he couldn't help thinking that if people had stuck together back there, worked together, maybe there could have been more survivors.

He glanced at Margaret, who was listening to what Mathew had to say, smiling at him, encouraging him to speak, and he found himself smiling again, realising all that mattered was the two of them getting to safety.

They would just look out for each other and to hell with the others. Yes, perhaps selfishness was the way forward.

He just couldn't believe it had taken him so long to admit it.

19

MARGARET

Margaret glanced at Keith and flashed him a smile, feeling sure that what they had seen in the last day or so was breaking his heart, as it was breaking hers.

It seemed the world had gone crazy and everybody in it. They had kind of expected something to happen, although not on this scale, because recently there had been so much madness, people arguing and fighting, suicides on the increase, so many unloved souls suffocating in the chaos. So much bad news going around, and during times like that she thought people would have pulled together, tried to help each other, but no, it just seemed to her that people were obsessed with bad intentions. Then again, she wondered if it was just her perspective on people, and perhaps she had started to notice the bad more because she was focusing on the negative side of human nature. However, everybody seemed to be looking for the worst in people, trying to find a reason to hate rather than to love, judging people, living in a cynical society.

She recalled there had been many a time when Keith had asked why people couldn't behave themselves, just help each other rather than want to kill each other.

But she had started to believe that life wasn't like that, had never been like that.

It seemed it was harder to be good than be bad.

And when they had sat in the train as everybody began to panic, the frustration and disbelief was so evident in Keith's eyes, his voice of reason failing him. He would often think his words spoke volumes and would make people listen, but she was so sure that words could never flag down irrationality, despite the fact that he had tried to so many times in the past.

She remembered the moment he had wanted to leave the train, to try and sort the situation, try and talk rational sense into people with no thought for his own safety. And if she hadn't been with him on the train he would have done, and therefore would more than likely have died, as those that were doing the killing were just barbaric, like all killers. But this was the first time in their lives they had witnessed something like this with their own eyes, seen what they so detested, realising a peaceful solution was way too much to ask for. No, you couldn't reason with those people, not with the devil. Perhaps, just perhaps, guns were the only answer for those sorts...

The thought was harrowing and she didn't want to believe it, didn't want to accept what she thought was possibly the logical solution. For far too long their beliefs had been against the gun, but what if they had been under an illusion; maybe sometimes guns were the only answer.

She looked at the others and recalled their harrowing stories, realising how people were more concerned about themselves and their loved ones than what was happening around them.

She would have considered those people selfish once, but not any more. They had their priorities right.

She felt for them all, and the reason she had tried to be as generous as she could was that she realised how lucky she was to have the one that mattered to her close by in such terrible times.

And when all this was over, when normality returned, it would be time for them to reconsider their lives and priorities. Possibly close the business, sell up and emigrate like they had always talked about doing, get away from it all, turn their backs on civilisation.

But first and foremost they had to get through the here and now, and she believed they would be able to do that. But they would have to work together, everybody in that room, as selfishness wouldn't help any of them and may destroy them, so together it would have to be – safety in numbers. Then again, it was selfishness that had kept them all alive. They were all cowards, they could have done something to help, but their own existence was more important. They could have helped that frail old woman, and she could have been there with them if they had acted differently. They were going to have to live with that thought.

20

LISA

Since Lisa had managed to find the sanctuary of the office, she had had the time to reflect on the nightmare, painfully recalling what she had been through, what she had failed to do. She had then found herself thinking over and over about how close her family had always been, always looking out for each other, always there for each other in a crisis, sitting around the table and talking things through until a solution was found. Her family was her mum, dad and Vicky, and of course her partner Wayne, and Wayne's family becoming a part of hers. True strong family unity. Her mum had always said how important that was, and Wayne's mum had said the same. The highlight of the week was when they all got together for dinner every Sunday, both families uniting as one, spending quality time together. They would begin at a country pub and have lunch, and end up at either parents' house until late in the evening, having to drag themselves away.

Her journey home with Wayne was usually carried out in silence, the radio unable to fill the void, missing the laughter, the closeness of family unity; priceless.

Priceless?

However, now her sister was dead, and her mum and dad were out there somewhere, along with Wayne, and as for Wayne's parents…

The whole family had been separated at a time when family unity should be most important, blown apart by sheer madness.

She tried to imagine what her mum and dad were doing. She imagined them barricaded in the house, hoping and praying their precious daughters were safe. No doubt they would be sat side by side, managing somehow to make a Horlicks, her dad being very inventive in times of crisis, both betting their daughters had stayed together, just like they had done all their lives, looking out for each other. Her dad had said that just a few days ago, while they were on their Sunday pilgrimage to the pub.

She imagined her parents thinking Wayne was with them as well, all huddled up, safe. They would be keeping their spirits up by talking about family unity and the precious memories they have of happy times, her mum always saying in times of crisis, always think of the family, the memories we have together, as they are the moments you live for. Only a few days ago, when they were all out together, Wayne had smiled at her, wanting to tell the whole family the good news. He wanted to announce it at dinner, but Lisa had told him to wait, to tell them the following Sunday, as she wanted to make it special, have time to think of a way to do it, but she secretly wanted to tell her sister first.

But as the fiction faded and the thought of what really happened hit her again, it left her feeling sickened with herself.

She realised how little her parents had known her. How little she had known herself. If she had had an ounce of dignity, of family pride and unity, she would have tried to save her sister, or died trying; they had been inseparable, just like her parents said.

But no, it wasn't to happen like that.

And the one who was supposed to protect her?

What was he doing?

Yes, where was Wayne?

Well, when it happened he would have been working in the city, on road construction; he would have been in the heart of it when the explosion happened.

She cursed herself for not trying to contact him before the second explosion, when she had the chance to make all the difference. Perhaps he would have raced over to them, and they could all have been safe now. Then again, had he survived the blast, and if so, had he managed to escape the crazed?

Had her parents survived?

Had Wayne's family survived?

And if they hadn't, she would be alone, with no family to turn to apart from distant relations, ones she had hardly ever seen.

The pain she was feeling in her leg was no match for the pain she was feeling within.

No match at all.

She was sure the others were judging her, and would ditch her if anything happened. But then why would they take her with them? She was a burden, so no doubt she would have to fight alone.

Die alone, just like her sister.

And the thought terrified her.

21

Day 2

EUSTON TUBE STATION

5.32 p.m.

They had remained in the office for a few hours, without anyone venturing out, all just having time for their thoughts, praying and hoping that by the time they left the room the rescue services would be around. And yet even though it seemed logical, they had a feeling of dread that it wasn't going to be that easy, a feeling that no help would come. The helicopter they had talked about, the one advising them to head for Parliament Hill, wasn't that encouraging. It made them wonder how dangerous the streets had become if the police or army weren't there. They sensed more hardship was ahead, with risks and chances to be taken, knowing they were probably going to have to rely on each other, trust each other. The thought of those crazed lurking about was a frightening one.

While they were in the room, Matthew did most of the talking, and he told Ron, Margaret and his mother about his various friends, the sort of people they were,

MELTDOWN

painting a colourful picture of them, talking with pride of understanding everything about them, though pausing every now and then to wonder what had happened to them, trying to understand without asking, trying to look grown-up.

Ron, Margaret and Mary tried their hardest to keep his spirits up, to keep the conversation positive, talking about future plans and hopes. They said they were sure his friends were fine, and Ron had a little banter with him about which football teams they supported.

But deep down they were all wondering what the future held for them, reflecting on things realistically, and the future looked bleak. As the hours passed, the air within the room had become stagnant, making conversation and patience harder to maintain. They were grateful, though, for the chocolate Jake handed around, the sugar keeping them stimulated enough to just about stay awake, apart from John, who had slept for a short while and remained drowsy.

John's dreams were plagued just like his thoughts, and yes, they were about Debbie; he was just unable to get her out of his mind. Then again, he was sure they were all plagued by some thought or another, all having worries, with loved ones out there somewhere. When they had all introduced themselves, they had pricked their consciences of good and bad memories, of their weaknesses, of situations that were out of their hands, their desperation to reach loved ones so evident in some of their stories. And desperation leads to irrationality, as was evident everywhere.

'Okay,' John said, hoping to mould them as a team again before they made their move in just under an hour. 'So when all this is over, what changes are you going to make to your life? You know, with the feeling of mortality looming?'

He knew it was a strong question, but he was intrigued as to what people would say, certain what he would do if he was lucky enough to survive.

He was curious to know what plagued the others' thoughts. He wanted to try to clear a few demons before they made a move, to see if anyone let slip how desperate they were to stay in their unity or to split up once they reached the surface. He had his doubts about some of them.

He knew the ones to keep an eye on, although he couldn't stop them, but more importantly he knew the ones he could rely on.

'Tough one,' Ron said, trying for a smile, wanting to be the first to get what was on his mind off his chest. 'If I'm still alive, I'll probably get myself a decent job, cut down on the booze and cigarettes, get myself a new motorbike, a decent one, and just generally sort my life out.'

He knew there were a thousand other tasks he would like to undertake, most more important than the ones he had named. Such as finding his Libby and helping her sort her life out, get her away from those so-called friends of hers, even if it meant asking her to move in with him. That was the most important. He so wanted to build bridges with her. And right then he longed for a cigarette and a drink.

'Restructure our lives, you know, sort out what matters and what doesn't,' Mary said, feeling sure there was no longer any point in planning too far ahead when you never know what the future holds.

She felt as if she was in hell. It was just a five- to ten-minute walk from where Jamie worked; ten minutes away from finding out if he was waiting there. That would give her some peace of mind, as she so desperately needed to know if he was there or not. That was the most important thing in her life right now.

'I think we shall appreciate life more. Not let little things bother us as much as they used to, not get bogged down with politics,' Keith said.

Margaret nodded her agreement and then added, 'Possibly book that holiday we've been promising ourselves for a few months now, what we were umming and aahing about a few days ago. Then take it from there.'

Keith nodded. 'Yes, it's just about us now, sweetheart.'

They shared a smile, both knowing what really mattered, feeling liberated for the first time in goodness knows how long. They clarified their thoughts and focused on what they truly desired for themselves. They were so eager to get out of the room, out of the situation, and get on with their lives. As far as Keith was concerned, to hell with the world. Yes, it was just going to be about them from now on; he was just annoyed it had taken something so disastrous to make him admit that.

'I'll get myself fixed up first, then work out what to do,' Lisa said, trying for a smile.

Yet she knew her life had been blown apart and would never be the same again. She was not sure where it would go from there, and she was not sure how to handle it. And as for the weight of guilt, it was so overwhelming, so suffocating.

She just felt like curling up in a corner and fading away; she just needed the time to try to get her head together.

'There is so much I have to do, and in so little time, but one step at a time,' Jake said, smiling at Emma and adding a wink.

Though he was sure that what they both so desperately needed right then was a proper fix, the desperation starting to show. Then he would be able to think clearly, plot their next move.

Emma just smiled. She had heard it all before and knew how he struggled to make that first step, and no doubt he would struggle again. However, she knew what she was going to do. She had been thinking about it for a while and it didn't involve Jake, unless he shocked her. But she doubted that.

They all glanced at John, waiting for him to confess what he was planning to do, what evils he was going to release.

He thought about what to say, with Debbie and all that, but felt it just wasn't right to say anything. Probably because he felt embarrassed by it, or perhaps because he wasn't sure how he really felt.

'There's so much I would like to change and do, but old habits are hard to break,' he said, smiling, trying to mask the emotional turmoil he was feeling.

They all stared at him, and some offered a smile, others a slight nod, after which they retreated into their own thoughts, back to where they were before, dwelling on what mattered to them, their own lives.

Mathew then began telling them his plans before going back to the radio and seeing if there was anything apart from interference.

John felt awkward and wished he had said a little more than he had, had made himself look like a typical policeman; he was eager to know their business, but so cagey when it came to his.

Had he lost their trust?

Their respect?

Would they therefore split up when they reached the surface?

Then again, there was a place he was desperate to get to, and he would be more than happy to turn his back on them in order to get there. Perhaps that's what he should do.

22

Day 2

EUSTON TUBE STATION

6.21 p.m.

'Should be getting dark now, dark enough for us to make our move,' Ron said, breaking the silence that had formed over the past half an hour.

He was eager to get out of the room, have a cigarette, hit the surface and possibly find somewhere where there was alcohol, the thought of the whisky he had left behind still haunting him.

'We could do with moving,' Jake said, getting to his feet and stretching, bones creaking. 'Man, I feel rough. And you must admit, the atmosphere is a little heavy as well. Kind of wears you out, gives you a banging headache.'

They all mumbled their agreement, all sick of being in the room with just a candle for light and warmth, especially as it was starting to get cold.

John got to his feet, glanced at them all, noticing how alert they had become, waiting for him to make a decision, looking up to him, relying on his judgment.

Then, just for a split second or two, he found himself wishing Debbie would look up to him like that instead of relying so much on Fiona's opinion and ideas. Then again, perhaps he was being hard on them; perhaps they had waited for him, prayed for him to come, but no, the one time Debbie might have desperately wanted him, he had failed.

He thought for a moment if it might be possible to head in her direction, as they were about three miles from the flat, and from there, Parliament Hill was about a ten-minute drive. They would have the cover of darkness, which would give him peace of mind, even if she wasn't there.

But how congested were the roads with abandoned vehicles?

And would they run into more of those crazed people?

And if he did decide to head for her apartment, would the others want to find their loved ones too? It would more than likely end in disaster, as they were bound to meet up with those murderers at some stage. Most of them wouldn't survive, and he still had the responsibility of representing law and order, still had his duty.

Yes, duty first.

That thought stung him, as it had been that way for him and Debbie for far too long, both their lives being about duty first. But he had a choice right now and he knew where his priorities lay. To hell with it, so it wasn't to be a direct route to Parliament Hill, but a slight detour. He wouldn't tell the others until they were in the car and on the move; that would save anyone else requesting any detours, and he could always make out he had to collect something just in case of any arguments.

'Well, man, you ready or what?' Jake asked, frowning.

John nodded. 'Sure.'

'But when we hit the surface, let me and Ron scout round first,' John said as they all got to their feet.

They glanced at each other briefly and agreed, none wanting to complain, just wanting to get out of there and hopefully to safety. They followed John out of the room.

Ever since the incident there had been a stillness about the tube station, a stillness which had taken a life form of its own. It was a menacing presence, seemingly everywhere, and had an icy effect on the soul, an unnatural feeling about it. A stillness that seemed to not belong there, as if it had forced itself upon everybody within the station, and on reaching the surface it was apparent there too, as if it had also taken siege to the city. Taken siege to it just like the crazed had, but not in a deadly way. Then again, perhaps it had always been there but they had failed to notice it, too wrapped up in their own worlds to see beyond.

As they stepped out of the Underground, John and Ron switched off their torches and briefly glanced at the others, telepathically letting them know to wait where they were. Then the two men stepped forward and glanced around, feeling disappointed, as nothing had really changed. There were still bodies lying around, but they had been stripped of clothing, looters having no shame. There was rubbish and twisted metal that was once cars and other vehicles as far as the eye could see; nothing had changed there. And every step they made, all they could see were trashed and stripped shops, all looted of their contents, apart from the few with the steel shutters down.

No, nothing much had changed.

Apart from one thing, one very minor detail – the digital camera had gone. Looters again.

John and Ron then headed along Euston Road in the direction of Euston station, the only source of light coming from the moon that shone bright, shining on the twisted metal, gutted shops and mutilated bodies scattered everywhere, the eerie sight of glazed eyes and mouths agape on the dead. There was no sign of life, but to their relief no sign of the crazed ones either. But they both had that eerie feeling as if they were being watched and it was unnerving. John gladly accepted a cigarette from Ron, who was already on his fourth since leaving the Underground.

'Kind of makes you wonder if we are the only ones left,' Ron said, glancing for a brief moment at the moonlit night. He felt cold. He recalled the way he had felt the last time he had made that statement – disappointed. He hoped what he had said wasn't true, wanted some reassurance from John.

But John just stared ahead, lost in his own thoughts.

'You alright, mate?' Ron asked, knowing how pathetic it sounded.

John tried for a smile, thinking about Debbie's apartment being only a ten-minute drive away, reliving the nightmare he had witnessed on the surface and how close he had been to her flat when he had headed for the police station in Islington, so fucking close. He should have driven straight to her rather than headed for the station.

'So I take it we're heading for Euston train station?' Ron said, breaking into his thoughts.

He wanted to be moving, feeling uncomfortable standing there, the silence so eerie and heavy, that feeling of being watched so intimidating.

'That's right,' John said, still staring into the distance.

He was wondering how bad it was where Debbie's flat was, and just wished he had considered she might be there rather than at the bank. What a fucking idiot he had been. He didn't want to think about who she might be with any more; the thought angered him.

'Let's go and get the others then, eh? We all might as well make the journey since it isn't too far away,' Ron said, noticing how dazed John looked.

He wanted to get moving quickly, the officer's state frightening him.

'Sure,' John replied, still lost in thought. Then, as they turned to head back to the others, he said, 'As regards us being the only ones left … I doubt it. More than likely they are all at Parliament Hill.'

Ron smiled. 'Yes, that's right. Just me being silly.'

'COME QUICKLY,' Jake shouted, standing thirty or so yards behind them. He was wide-eyed, not sure what to do.

'Shit!' John said, gripping his gun as he ran, expecting the worst.

Ron tried to keep up, baton ready.

They both raced as fast as they could, preparing themselves for the worst, not sure how they were going to get out of it, just letting the adrenalin do the talking.

'Mary has gone, took off with her son,' Jake said, spitting his words out.

'Why didn't you try to stop her?' Ron snapped.

'Eh, man, chill out. I can't stop her from doing what she wants to do,' Jake said, backing off.

'You should have tried,' Ron said, pushing past him and heading back in the direction of the others as fast as he could, pavement pounding underfoot, tripping over bodies and discarded possessions.

Keith, Margaret and Emma were standing around, while Lisa was leaning against a wall. They were all looking at each other, wanting somebody to blame.

'What direction did she go in?' Ron asked, being the first to return by a few seconds.

'She kept saying something about where her husband worked,' Keith said, looking a little stressed.

'We told her to wait, but she just wouldn't listen. I even attempted to go after her, but she still wouldn't listen. She was hell-bent on heading for her husband's place of work,' Margaret said, eyes wide.

'And which direction was that?' Ron snapped.

Margaret pointed in the direction she had gone, towards Gower Street.

'She just wouldn't listen to reason,' Keith added.

Ron looked away, not wanting to look at any of them; they were all guilty as far as he was concerned.

'We have to find her,' he said a second later, turning to face them.

They all looked at each other, uncertainty in their eyes.

'Well?' Ron said, glancing at John, expecting him at least to show his support since he was supposed to represent law and order.

'Okay,' John said finally. His plans would have to be put on hold, and he cursed them all under his breath.

'Hang on a minute,' Jake said, stepping forward.

'Have you a problem with that?' Ron snapped. 'Have any of you a problem with that?' he added, daring somebody to speak, gripping the baton.

'I never said I had a problem,' Jake said, backing away again. 'Just think we should think things through, not go barging in the direction she went. I mean, she could have been killed and they could be waiting for us.'

'Have you always been a selfish bastard?' Ron snapped, hating the youth every time he looked at him, so reminding him of everything that was wrong with his daughter's friends.

'Let's just find her, eh?' Keith said, wanting to calm them all down before they attracted unwanted guests.

'It's just that Lisa ain't fit for too much walking,' Jake said, reminding them how they had had to help her from the office.

Margaret and Keith had been the ones to support her, making a fuss of her like she was their own daughter.

Ron glanced at Lisa, then the others, and disappeared back down the Underground, returning minutes later with a wheelchair.

And while John and Ron helped Lisa into the chair, Jake said to the others, 'You do realise that hot-headed twat is going to get us all killed?'

Keith and Margaret shared a look, neither complaining, just wanting peace. There was already too much disaster around them without creating more friction. Emma just grasped Jake's hand.

They all then followed John and Ron, who led them in the direction they said Mary had gone. Gower Street was a very long street and she could have headed down a side street, so they could easily lose track of her. They remained fully alert, constantly glancing around at the looming buildings, looking so gloomy in the moonlight, most having been broken into, bodies lying outside. They all felt as if they were being watched, the slightest noise sending their hearts racing, all reliving the horrors they had witnessed the previous day.

'There,' Ron said, gripping John's arm and pointing down Grafton Way.

They hadn't had to go that far after all.

Mary was stood glancing up at a building, clutching her son's hand, plucking up the courage to enter.

They all hurried over to her, and allowed Ron to speak.

'Mary, why? You could get both of you killed,' he said, his voice soft as he moved closer. He was tempted to place his hand on her shoulder, but chose not to.

'My husband, he works here,' she said, not taking her eyes off the building.

The huge window was smashed, the double doors wide open; it was four storeys high, and had been modified from the inside, with flats either side.

'This looks bad,' John said, stepping forward, knowing it could be even worse inside.

Her husband could be pretty cut up, and there could be some of those crazed things in there, just waiting.

Just fucking waiting to pounce!

'We should go,' he added.

Mary ignored John's suggestion and stepped forward, entering the building with her son. Unfazed by what John had said, the urge to be with Jamie was overwhelming rationality.

John and Ron glanced at each other, looking for courage, before following her, knowing deep down this spelt trouble and could be very serious. John was the first to enter, both with weapons ready.

The reception area had been trashed and there was blood near the front desk. Tables and chairs had been smashed, signs that an obvious battle had taken place. And just like the Underground and the rest of London, there was an eeriness about the place.

Mary broke the stillness that had formed by striding over the debris and heading for the stairwell, crunching glass underfoot, in the direction of where her husband worked.

Ron and John followed, both not speaking, looking for any sign of life while bracing themselves for a possible battle, a battle they were expecting.

They climbed the stairwell to the next floor and stepped into a room, which once housed computers and other hardware, all of which had disappeared; desks had been overturned, drawers emptied, contents on the floor. Obvious signs of looters, or blind panic as people fled.

Ron paused as he saw something near his foot – a photo. He picked it up and found himself staring at a younger Mary with a baby in her arms, baby Mathew. He then noticed another picture and picked that one up too, seeing her husband standing with another woman, a dark-haired, wealthy-looking woman. They were in a bar, perhaps a hotel bar. Both smiling. The photo appeared to be recent.

He glanced at Mary, who was staring at him inquisitively, wanting to know what he had picked up.

He gave her the picture of herself, but not the one of her husband with the other woman; no, that one went in his pocket.

John and Ron surveyed the room and saw that there had been no orderly withdrawal, but bedlam, like everywhere else; every man for himself. And even possible death as some tried to flee, as there were suited men just outside the building.

There just seemed no escape from the violence.

No escape at all.

'Take a seat here,' Keith said, resurrecting a chair that was near the reception desk.

'Thanks,' Lisa said, trying for a smile, but the pain in her leg was so overwhelming.

Her leg had swollen, so it took all of her energy to shuffle from the entrance to the chair.

But she managed another smile and added, 'Thanks for pushing me in the chair, really sweet of you.'

'Eh, no problem,' Keith said, smiling.

Margaret smiled too, both only too happy to oblige, to be able to do something for somebody else in a time of madness, show a little love, love they were sure she needed.

'This is fucking ridiculous. It's obvious that fucking Ron has the hots for her and wants to bang her one,' Jake said, appearing at the side of the others, looking around the ransacked reception area, breathing heavily, perspiration on his face, so desperate for his fix. The disappointment was evident in his eyes; this was not the route he had hoped they would take, and his plan was in tatters.

'There is still compassion in this world, even if you think it doesn't exist,' Margaret said, her eyes warning him. She felt tired with the angry little boy's attitude.

Jake glanced at her. An ageing has-been, that's if she had ever been anybody, which he doubted. Not worth the hassle.

'Well, if we continue to hang around here we are going to end up like most of them out there,' Jake said, glancing out of the open doors at the corpses.

He noticed the lock had been smashed off and wondered if the doors had been forced open by those trying to get in or those trying to get out. The thought terrified him.

'Don't worry, son, we shall be away soon and all this will be a memory,' Keith said, trying to do what he had done most of his life and keep the peace. Knowing they would be together for a little while longer, he wanted to keep it sweet.

'And a bad one at that,' Lisa said, trying to fight the pain.

Jake turned away from the others, too tired to argue, Emma at his side. He headed in the direction of the door and lit a cigarette, the first in what seemed like a lifetime, though his seventh since hitting the surface, needed just as much as the others. And while he smoked it, he stared out at the dead, looking at the poor bastards, wondering who they were and if he had seen any of them before. Then again, they were probably the sort of people that would look down on Jake and Emma, so perhaps they deserved what had happened to them. He allowed himself to smile. Yes, that was right, they deserved what had happened to them.

Margaret, Keith and Lisa shared a look, knowing there would always be one bad apple in the cart. Emma watched, feeling a little isolated, not sure who to feel for, though she felt weak and irritated from the cold sweats and cramps that were taking hold of her. Margaret commented on how ill she looked.

'SHIT!' Jake said, hoping and praying he was seeing things, hoping it was the symptoms of heroin withdrawal.

'Jake?' Emma said, eyes wide, expecting the worst.

He didn't reply and just stared, unsure what to do. There were about four of them, and they were heading their way, running like hell, so eager to get at them, seeming to have appeared from nowhere.

Jake turned to face Emma and the others, the cigarette falling from his mouth. He noticed them looking as startled as he was, all expecting something but completely unaware of what he had seen, of what was coming their way.

'They...' he managed, before the force of one of the crazed men sent him flying towards them, crashing to the ground.

'Oh God,' Lisa gasped as she saw them enter, looking like they had just come from hell, snarling like wolves, clothes wet and clinging to them, and their eyes immediately upon her, burning like hell. Yet she felt calm, ready for them, visions of her sister in her mind. Then within a flash, two of them had pounced on her, both with hands full of the broken glass for weapons.

She just closed her eyes, gasping as they slashed her, saying a prayer with her sister on her mind.

Keith immediately rushed over and pulled one of the men away, only to find himself the target. He wrestled with the man, their hands locked, trying to control him, hoping he would calm down but deep down knowing it was either him or the monster who was going to die.

'Shout for John and Ron,' Keith shouted, looking in the direction of Jake and Emma, who were just watching, not sure what to do, shocked by what they were witnessing.

Margaret was torn between helping Keith and shouting for help, the whole affair overwhelming her, tears streaming down her face.

As he fought, Keith noticed the other two crazed people were staring at Jake, Emma and Margaret, possibly seconds away from launching an attack on them, and all Keith could do was watch while he grappled with the man who was hell-bent on killing him. And as for the noise, all he could hear was Lisa choking and gasping for breath.

'Margaret, go, save yourself!' Keith shouted as the man began to overpower him and force him to the ground.

He knew the danger Margaret was in, but all she could do was stand and stare, feeling confused, a clash of right and wrong colliding.

Jake gripped Emma's hand and gave her arm a little tug so he could get her attention.

'Let's go, otherwise these fuckers are going to kill us,' he said.

And before she could reply, he led her in the direction of the stairwell.

'My husband needs our help,' Margaret protested as they went, stunned.

'We should take her with us,' Emma said, pausing for a moment, noticing how distressed she was.

'NO, DON'T LEAVE, KEITH NEEDS OUR HELP, PLEASE,' Margaret shrieked.

'No, come on,' Jake said, noticing her heading for her husband, blind to the two other crazed heading her way, all destined to die.

'What is going on?' John asked, pausing on the stairs.

Ron was behind him, and he saw Jake at the bottom of the stairwell, white and clammy, unable to speak.

'They're being attacked,' Emma managed, tears streaming down her face.

John and Ron looked at each other before rushing down past Jake and Emma, and into the reception area.

Two crazed men were attacking Margaret while she just lay fitting, hitting her with shards of glass and anything they could lay their hands on. Lisa was lifeless, blood everywhere. As for Keith, he was still wrestling with one of them, crying.

John immediately shot the two dead who were attacking Margaret and then killed the other two.

And as the ringing of the shots faded, John and Ron sighed.

Mary, Mathew, Jake and Emma suddenly appeared at their side. Mary, though, led her son back the way they had come, shielding him from the bloodshed.

'Seal the door,' John said, grabbing the receptionist desk.

Ron grabbed the other end and helped him carry it, fumbling and stumbling with it as they carried it over the corpses.

They closed the doors and then placed it in front.

John turned to Jake and said, 'I want you to stand here and let us know if you see anything; at least that will give us a little time to act.'

Jake hesitated, still dazed by what had happened, reliving the nightmare in his mind, the sound of the shots still gripping him.

'Do it now!' Ron said, snapping into his thoughts.

Ron helped Keith to his feet, who rushed over to his wife and crouched down by her side.

She was bleeding from her mouth and nose, and there was blood oozing out of her side, her clothes drenched in it, her eyes looking a little dilated; however, she was conscious.

'Oh, what have they done to you? What have they done to you?' Keith murmured, taking her in his arms.

'Oh, Keith…' she managed, choking on the blood in her mouth. She tried for a smile. 'What … a state to be in … eh?'

Keith kissed her on her crown, telling her how much he loved her.

She tried for another smile, but found it hard, the pain she was feeling overwhelming her. Then she found herself wondering if this was the end for her, knowing there was something seriously wrong with her from the blood and the light-headed sensation she was feeling. She was finding it extremely hard to breathe, yet her heart was beating like mad. Her vision distorting every now and then as the colours became one mass white. What she was experiencing gripped her, terrified her.

She tried hard to consider what she wanted to tell Keith, trying to sum up everything she felt for him in as few words as she could, knowing she didn't have the energy to say too much, though wanting to give him courage and support to go on in the face of what was sure was the end for her.

With what energy she did have, though, she placed a hand on his cheek and, as she looked into his eyes, she smiled.

She whispered, 'I … I love you.'

Keith hugged her and told her the same, and continued to tell her, crying into her shoulder.

Ron and John glanced at each other, both wanting to blame somebody, so wishing they could get their hands on those responsible.

They glanced at Lisa's lifeless body, deciding to give her a little dignity by moving her body to one of the other rooms on the next floor, and covered her with a blanket they had found. Then they collected the bodies of the four John had shot and placed them in another room. Both pausing for a moment, they noticed they just looked like ordinary people, like the average hard-working person. And they had names, had had a life before whatever happened had sent them crazy. So much sorrow and pain, so much senseless slaughter, but why?

John glanced at Ron and told him to comfort Mary while he returned to the reception area, not wanting to remain there any longer. He felt so low for having killed them, and that they would probably have to remain in the building for the night.

'There was no other way, you know. If you hadn't, they would have killed us all,' Ron said.

'Sure,' John said, unconvinced. He wondered what could possibly go wrong next.

23

MARY

Mary stared again at the photo, feeling warmth towards it; it was one of her favourite pictures of them, taken nearly a decade ago, back when they were on holiday. Mathew had been just one, and it was his first time abroad. It had been a blissful week in Greece, celebrating his first birthday, and they had both said how it had possibly been the best holiday they had ever had, with so many precious memories; their first holiday as a family. How fast time had slipped away since then, but she could remember it like it was yesterday. Yes, that holiday had meant so much to both of them. That was why he had carried the picture around with him, to remind him of the reason he worked, to spend more quality time with his family, and how he had been promising to do that, but recently it had just been words; that's all, just words.

She glanced at his silver pen, his lucky pen. He would always fill out his forms with it and took pride in using it, as she had bought it for him. Then there was the gleaming penny, his good luck charm; he would always crease his letters with it, saying it would seal luck.

Apart from the picture she had found near the desk Jamie worked at, there were a few other items she had picked up which she was not aware of. He was a member of an expensive health club, and she wondered why he had kept that a secret. Then there was a diary listing expensive restaurants and hotels he had obviously been using; perhaps he used them all for business, as he had often said how the bank was planning on expanding, and attracting investors can be expensive.

She then focused on the photo, pen and lucky penny again, knowing he had always carried them around with him, said he kept them on the desk in front of him, said he would never go anywhere without them.

But they were with Mary and where was he?

Had they all been evacuated?

Or had it been like everywhere else, a free for all?

No time to think, just flee.

And if that was the case, had he headed for their house?

The thought of him heading back to their house had gone through her mind more than once. But she didn't want to believe it and had tried to nonsense the thought, but it was entering her mind more frequently now. Well, she hoped he had not. She imagined it had got a hell of a lot worse not long after they had left the neighbourhood. She imagined those crazed things rampaging through the houses, smashing and ransacking the residents' possessions, murdering anyone and everyone who got in their way, just like her neighbours.

And it seemed the deranged people were everywhere.

But why were these people behaving like that?

It was as if they had gone mad; rabies or something...

Perhaps it was something to do with the green atmosphere.

But if that was the case, why hadn't it affected them too?

And after everything she had heard and listened to from the others, she felt more confused than ever before. No answers, and no sign of it coming to an end.

What must the others think of her selfish act? If it had not been for her, Margaret and Lisa would still be alive. And not forgetting risking her son's life again. If she hadn't been so selfish they could all have been safe now at Parliament Hill, sitting around a table, raising a glass and toasting to their safety, and there might have been a chance that Jamie was waiting there for her; perhaps all their relatives would have been sitting with them, all toasting together, and all having a sombre moment for those that had been murdered, even shedding a tear for them.

The others must hate her, and rightfully so.

'Mum, what is going to happen to us? And where is Dad?' Mathew asked, breaking into her thoughts, sounding exhausted, the whole event catching up with the young man.

She kissed him on the crown, again realising how lucky they had been, because if the others hadn't joined them, she and Mathew would more than likely have been killed by those things.

Margaret and Lisa's life in trade for theirs. How cruel life was.

She silently cursed herself again for her own stupidity, and yet she knew she had had to do it.

'Well, Mum?' Mathew asked, wanting answers to his questions.

'We are going to leave this building in the morning and get ourselves rescued,' Mary said, hoping it would be as simple as that.

'But what if we meet more of those mad men and women?' Mathew asked, eyes upon her, wanting so many answers.

'We'll hide until they go,' Mary said, not sure what she would do.

'But what if they come after us? And why are they angry?' Mathew asked.

'I don't know, love, I just don't know. Now, why don't you just go to sleep, eh?' Mary said, not wanting to think any more, his questions provoking memories of the whole entire mess, a mess into which she seemed to have dug them all deeper.

'But what about Dad?' Mathew said.

'He would have been evacuated with all the other workers, and no doubt he is waiting for us somewhere,' Mary said, hoping that was how it was, hoping and praying everything would work out come the following day.

'He might have gone home looking for us, though,' Mathew said, reminding her of the thoughts that had been tormenting her. 'He might even have gone to Auntie's, thinking we are there.'

She so wanted to give some logical reason why he wouldn't have done that, but the truth was he could be as irrational as her when he wanted to be; love does make you do crazy things.

'It is a possibility, but I doubt it,' she said, trying to sound reassuring.

Then, as Mathew lay his head on her lap, she glanced in the direction of Ron who was sat opposite and said silently, 'I'm so sorry.'

Ron just returned the smile.

Mary wished he could have been a little more sympathetic, as the smile didn't look convincing. But deep down she didn't blame him, didn't blame any of them for hating her, as she was to blame for the deaths of Margaret and Lisa; well, that was how she felt. And she would have to live with that for the rest of her life.

What she dreaded most was that if Jamie had gone to their house looking for them, she would have *his* death on her conscience as well, and that she wouldn't be able to cope with.

It was going to be a long night for her, a very long night.

24

RON

Ron had listened to Mary trying to reassure her son and was more than tempted to add his reassurance, but hadn't because he realised he didn't really know them, and it would have seemed like he was pushing himself upon them, even though he felt as if he had known them for what seemed like a lifetime. Then again, when you see the tender side to somebody you tend to be drawn to them quickly. But they had more than likely been nice to him for survival reasons only, and if they had found her husband, she would have been right there looking up to him, Ron long forgotten, second best again. He couldn't blame her, though, as he was obviously an intelligent man, working for a little investment bank like this. He imagined he probably made buckets of money, not like Ron, and also had a huge ego, especially with his fancy woman. *How disgusting that was*, Ron thought, and he knew exactly how it was all going to end.

So second best he was to a Casanova, and like he had said before, it wouldn't be the first time, and possibly not the last; second best to his ex-wife's husband and second best to Libby's friends.

It seemed when it came to people he was jinxed, always coming off worst. He recalled when he was alone with Mary and Mathew in the staffroom back in King's Cross, and when it came to the important conversation, about families, how he had stumbled, as family life had always been a disaster for him. Then he recalled when he had heard she had gone off with her son, and it just seemed as if she couldn't wait to get away from him. It reminded him of so many other people that had passed through his life; then again, perhaps he was the problem, had always been the problem. He did have annoying habits, had upset far too many work colleagues and overheard so-called friends talking about his annoying ways while he was out drinking, saying how he didn't know what he was talking about and would often never listen. Boring snoring Ron. Could he blame her for wanting to escape boring old Ron?

Suddenly, he became tempted to break into a laugh, wondering why he had been acting like a lovesick teenager towards Mary.

He asked himself whether he was that lonely, that he would try to make a hero out of himself to gain a ready-made family.

Or perhaps he had been doing it to prove a point.

Prove he wasn't the loser his wife thought, everybody in his world thought. That he wasn't just out for number one, and there was more to him than football, bikes and beer.

He told himself he was a caring person, looking out for his daughter, even though he had failed to be with her right now.

He sighed. He felt like kicking himself once again, because he could have so easily reached her when it had all first kicked off, but no, cowering in the staff room was his ideal plan; bury his head in the sand and hope it would just sort itself out, shirking from responsibility, just like always.

And he had failed to break away from the others and go looking for her; that was why he wasn't with her. He could have found himself a motorbike and searched the city for her ... he still could; be the true man, be the hero Libby wanted him to be.

Perhaps he would. Although it would be risky, it would be the right thing to do, to prove he was a caring person, prove he was still Libby's hero, even though it had been many long years since he had played the hero, if he ever really had. He should also probably check up on a few friends as well, do the rounds; he did have a heart after all.

He watched as Mary let Mathew lie across her lap and try to sleep while she ran her hand through his hair.

Her eyes upon him, smile on her face, motherly bond so strong.

Then, as she glanced in his direction and silently said how sorry she was, he offered her a smile, hoping it looked reassuring. He believed it wasn't her fault, just a chain reaction of events, one disaster after another, just like everything in life. Just like his life. And anyway, she just wanted what they all did — to reach her loved one. Even though she had taken risks to do so, big risks, Ron was so sure he would have done the same if he thought his daughter had been just a street away. And he was sure the others would have done the same too, and that was one thing he admired her for, the risks she had taken to try and reach her loved one, again reminding him that he should have tried. Should he?

But it was no good thinking like that. He had to believe Libby was safe, and he was sure that just like him, the others hoped and prayed they would find their loved ones, and he was sure they would. On a positive note at least, Ron and what remained of their group were the lucky ones so far, as they were still alive, still had hope.

Yes, so far so good.

He then wondered how many of his friends were still alive.

Wondered how they were coping.

He recalled Barry, lying there with the iron bar, obviously having fought to his last breath like a true hero.

But he wasn't hiding any more; in fact, he had been an unlikely hero. And he had decided he would not let Mary and Mathew down, and was going to get them both to safety.

Show the world he wasn't a loser and somehow check on his daughter's place as well.

He allowed himself a smile, because that was what he was going to do, and he would do so even if it cost him his own life.

That's what good people do, put others first, just like Barry. Then there would be no regrets, not like the regrets he had seen in Lisa's eyes. No, he couldn't live with that burden, so action it must be.

25

JAKE

Jake had considered over and over again if he should and could have done anything to prevent the death of Margaret and Lisa. He had gone over and over it in his mind, but it had all happened so fast, like a blur, basic instinct kicking in. And it did sicken him to think he didn't do anything but save himself.

But the truth was, he had been too frightened to act, far too frightened to stand up to those things. Then again, he had never liked confrontation of any kind; that was why he let Emma make their money, let Emma steal from folk while he would be the diversion, but if the truth be known, he hated himself for being so weak, and he knew he had to overcome it otherwise he would lose her.

He then recalled the look in Emma's eyes. Disappointment was hard to disguise, and he had seen the look more than once. He knew that unless he changed, she would flash him that look again and again, and possibly keep on doing so until finally, she realised she could do without him. And he dreaded that day, as he knew his hold on her was getting weaker.

He thought again about what they had seen since the situation started, the shops being looted, personal belongings being stolen and how easy it was for him to steal, just walk into a shop and take what he wanted, just like he had always dreamed of doing and was sure everybody dreamed of. And what he dreaded most was that in the next day or so it would all be over, as it would then be back to the streets, scrounging again, cursing they hadn't acted while they had the chance, hadn't taken advantage of the situation. Then again, he would have done if it wasn't for the policeman; how he hated him.

However, what if he could still gain something from the disaster? He had planned to flee earlier, heading for Euston train station or one of the bus stations, slipping away and having a go at hitting a few shops. Then he would have proven to Emma that he could do something amazing and manly; he would have surprised her, taken control for once, proved his life was not just about him.

And there were nothing more in the world he was sure would make her happy than that, and he so wanted to, just to show her how much he cared. That would hopefully take away those many moments of disappointment and doubt, and restore some much-needed faith; he owed her that.

He then considered if one or two of the drug dealers he knew had been killed, some of those people that had pissed him off, rubbed his nose in it for far too long, those he would love to have killed. Smirking when they were taking the money off them, being all polite and kind, then when they owed them they came after them like hell hounds, demanding their fucking money, with a relentless barrage of abuse, threatening to kneecap them until they got it.

They were the scum in his eyes, the people responsible for the shit state of affairs Emma and him were in. They had ruined his life, ruined Emma's life.

And if anything had happened to those dealers, it would be a pity to see all those drugs go to waste. Jake could start up his own empire, be in the driving seat for a change. And not forgetting those drugs dealers' nest eggs of banknotes they had tucked away; it would be a pity to let it all go to waste.

And anyway, some of that money was rightfully his.

Then he recalled once again when they were in the shop and he stole the chocolate and cigarettes, that burning desire to rob the till, and he would have done if it hadn't been for the two do-gooders with him. Yes, it had been bugging him. And who would have known, who would have cared?

How many other shops were there to rob that hadn't been robbed or looted? There must still be a couple of thousand out there.

London was a city of rich pickings, just waiting for someone to collect.

There were obviously scroungers about, as they had taken that digital camera, and robbed the dead of their clothes and money. If he didn't act soon it would be too late; second best again, back on the streets as broke as when it all started, though this time he could be alone.

So what he needed was a plan, and a fucking good one.

And boy, was he going to think of one.

He took out a cigarette and lit it. Cigarettes always helped him to think, but like before, if only he had a joint, he would definitely think clearer and sharper, but he was pleased about one thing – at least he had had his fix.

26

EMMA

Emma found herself feeling revolted by the man she was sitting next to, the man that just could not see beyond his own existence. She found it so hard to believe that he had left Margaret, Keith and Lisa to defend for themselves, knowing they didn't stand a chance, as she was sure that if they had both tried their hardest, they may all have lived; they may have held them off long enough until John and Ron arrived and therefore all got out of there alive.

But no, that wasn't Jake's way, it had never been Jake's way; Jake's way was about saving his skin and that was all it had ever been about. As long as he was fine, to fuck with the rest.

She recalled the many times when they were out pickpocketing, knowing it was down to Emma to snatch the purse from the handbag, to walk into a man and quickly slip his wallet out of his pocket while she apologised, and what would Jake be doing? Nothing but fleeing once she had done the deed, encouraging her to follow, just eager to get his hands on what she had stolen.

She then thought about how the rest of the group had looked after each other in the crisis; Ron looking out for

Mary, Keith and Margaret being so kind to Lisa, and Margaret being kind to everyone, showing true humanity in a time of selfishness. If it hadn't been for the policeman, would he have stayed with her in the Underground? She couldn't help but wonder whether, if they hadn't met up with him and had run into some of those crazed things, he would have used her for bait while he escaped.

Perhaps, or perhaps not.

Then again, perhaps she was being too hard on him.

Although, if there was one thing the crisis had done, it had made her admit to herself where she had been going wrong, and when it was all over she was going to move on.

Yes, move on, as in the words of her mum. She had said she could do better, a hell of a lot better, and perhaps she was right, perhaps she had always been right.

She would find someone who was a decision maker, who would look out for her, support her, be strong for her, help her kick the habit Jake had inflicted upon her – even though she had a fond relationship with drugs – and more than anything a man who would be willing to help others in times of crisis. One of the reasons she had been planning to train as a nurse or a counsellor was to help others, not rob them like Jake had taught her to do.

No more stumbling from one crisis to another, no more living outside of the law, having to make money for the both of them.

She felt sure that right then they were being judged by the others and that they had been labelled as wasters, a label she so hated.

She glanced at Jake and suddenly found herself feeling frustrated with herself and him, wishing, so wishing he would make a decision, stand up and be a man, show a little tenderness when it came to others. Shock her by showing he would be prepared to get his head out of the sand when the time came and think beyond his own existence.

She prayed he would.

She prayed like she had done many times that he would prove her wrong, prove to her that she hadn't wasted her life by being with him, hadn't spent those awful hours with those sweaty men in hotels for nothing.

Just for once she hoped he'd surprise her, just the once; prove that she wasn't being too hard on him.

Then at least he would take away the frustration she was feeling, restore her faith in him, because perhaps she was being hard on him.

No, she had told herself he would have to prove otherwise. And she would only give him until the end of the crisis to prove himself, otherwise it was goodbye.

Goodbye for good.

27

KEITH

Keith had continued to hold Margaret long after she died and sang the record she loved so much, The Carnival, over and over again, just mumbling each line, skipping from one line to the next, just like an old scratched '45 on a record player, jumbled, but not missing out the main lines; kind of like his memories of their life together, returning thick and fast, with one particular recent memory, only days old, a memory filled with optimism and excitement, though both had died along with Margaret. The long weekend in Paris they were planning, the city she loved so much, a city for the romantics, for the dreamers and lovers.

They had been talking about it for most of Monday, and the more they had talked, the more excited they had become.

They would see a show while there, as they were both fluent in French, one for the romantics, a super-charged one with a breathtaking finish, one that leaves you with a lump in your throat, tears in your eyes, a warm feeling within, just undiluted nourishment for the soul, and restores your faith in humanity. They would then round off a super weekend in a small family-run restaurant, one they had heard so much about, eating by candlelight and the owners treating you like you were one of their own, nothing too much trouble.

What a weekend that would have been.

And they were no strangers to Paris, having visited many years ago, and once upon a time they had links with a socialist movement there and so would be often visiting, but recent trips were more for romance and art, priceless times.

And they were also planning to visit a few museums they had not yet been to, including one that had recently opened and was hosting an art expedition, showing the works of up-and-coming artists, artists that were not afraid to express themselves no matter how shocking their work may be. Margaret was a big fan of art, especially French art, and she had so many books and replica pictures of contemporary French artists, saying they were masters of passion, not afraid to express their work through nudity or the crueller side of humanity, like the Holocaust.

They were in the travel agents only two days ago, sat in there all Sunday afternoon. The lady had patiently gone through brochure after brochure with them, the three of them drinking coffee while making small talk, the lady trying to find them the best deal, the best hotel closest to all the attractions. All of them laughing and joking. Margaret explaining to the lady what they intended to do and how much they intended to fit in to the trip, then telling her of previous trips they had been on to Paris, though not discussing the political side, as they were sure nobody was interested in that; it had taken them a lifetime to realise that. The lady, in her thirties, seemed captivated by their stories.

He then recalled them taking the brochures away with them, promising to go through them some time in the week. They had taken the lady's card, and she had told them that on deciding, to get back to her, as she was excited about booking their trip. Margaret assured her they would return the following Sunday.

But life wasn't about returns.

No, not at all. It was about decisions and chances, it was about being reflective, gaining positives from negatives and using them in the present, facing each situation head-on; well, that is what Keith believed. But what was there left for him to believe? It all seemed so messed up, and there were certainly no positives to be gained from the negatives.

The thought was deflating, heartbreaking and suffocating.

He then considered the people that had attacked his Margaret.

Why had they done it?

Why?

What had she ever done wrong to deserve what had happened to her, when she had devoted her life to helping others?

And the one question he dreaded was, how was he going to carry on without her?

How was he going to carry on without his Margaret? He had never done anything without her.

The thought terrified him.

The youthfulness in him had died along with Margaret; it was as if he was dying, everything good within him dying, darkness and decay descending on him so fast, suffocating him.

He felt like a frightened child for the first time in his adult life, a feeling he hated and was sure he wouldn't be able to live with.

No, there was no way forward for him any more.

28

JOHN

John was staring out at the outside world and had been doing so for quite a while, a world so silent and cold, dark and eerie, and yet peaceful, an unreal peacefulness. He imagined that was what it was like after a huge battle of old, the silence giving you time to reflect on those you had killed, those you could and should have saved, the thoughts tiring, depressing and disheartening. He tried to gain a little solace from a cigarette or two.

He tried to think back to when things were as normal as he could ever imagine. Only three days ago, though it seemed like years, the roads would have been gridlocked with tourist buses, taxis and day trippers, all wanting a glimpse of the historical city, wanting to take in as much as they could, capture the atmosphere, most armed with cameras, wanting to record what they were witnessing, so much to take in, plenty of fond memories, and no doubt by the end of the evening they would be feeling worn out. Leaving the hustle and bustle behind, so glad to not be living in the city. Feeling sorry for those that did, John being one of them, and like himself, most of his fellow residents would have been trying to get through the hustle and bustle which was an everyday occurrence, trying to survive in a city that was getting dearer to live in. Then again, the whole country was suffering, the whole world, the global recession gripping all.

Recession?

The fucking recession.

He smiled to himself, thinking of himself like old Bill, groaning away. He so hoped he had survived. But old Bill was right; the house prices had collapsed, the commodity slump, evaporation of equity, people losing their jobs and those with jobs having to cut back on their hours, their lifestyle, and those with no job losing everything. So much anger and frustration, was it a surprise that this had happened? It was bound to, just the way old Bill had said many a time. And right now all that was left was devastation, terror and fear. He hoped, so hoped they had seen the worst, and he was sure there were millions out there thinking the same.

But where were those that had survived, the hard-working law-abiding Londoners?

He glanced out at the flats, the hotels; perhaps they were imprisoned inside, wondering what their next move was going to be, too scared to venture out. They had probably watched the horror unfold in the bank he now stood in, trembling behind the blinds, the minority taking over, streets under siege with the unruly, all wondering when help was going to come, when it was all going to get better, when things would change, but feeling for sure things would only get worse.

John smiled. Ironically, it seemed that nothing had changed, society the same as usual; just fucking stinks.

He then thought about what options they would have when dawn arrived, either head in the direction they had been advised to, or to hell with the rest and head for Debbie's apartment.

The second option was tempting, even though he thought she probably wouldn't be there, and might be at Parliament Hill.

Parliament Hill?

He then recalled a few days earlier, Friday to be precise, old Bill had mentioned something about Parliament Hill being sealed off, the army doing an exercise up there; a coincidence perhaps?

However, he still had to go to her apartment, just in case, and the thought he dreaded entered his mind again. What if she was dead?

And they may be ambushed by a dozen or more of those mad bastards, so it could turn out to be an ill-fated mission, just like the one Mary had led them to and of course the millions out there that had possibly been slaughtered, their crime, just trying to reach those they cared about.

Could he take that chance?

Should he take that chance?

But she could be alive, waiting for him.

He had a feeling though that morale was low and that whatever they decided to do, things could go wrong come the following day, and more than likely would. So what difference would it make if they took one more chance?

Just a ten-minute drive away.

It would give him peace of mind.

And after the insane actions the rest of the group had pulled, they did owe him one, and his wasn't going to be all that insane. They could all remain in the motor while he visited her flat, and if they didn't want to wait they could leave him, just drop him off. And even if they did wait and the worst should happen, they could always drive away. He was sure he could survive; he was good at that.

He allowed himself a smile, knowing what he was going to do, what mattered to him. And that was all that did matter, personal choice over duty, the way it should always be, should have always been and always will be from then on. Well, that was what he told himself. He lit another cigarette, a kind of celebration smoke.

29

Day 3

C.A.S. INDEPENDENT BANKING CENTRE GRAFTON WAY

7.03 a.m.

John had remained awake the entire evening; then again, he had remained awake for almost two days. He had napped while they were sat in the Underground, but his dreams had been exhausting, with visions of those that wanted his help screaming out, cursing him as he ran past them, his father laughing, before stating what a waste of space John was.

But he did need rest, as his limbs felt extremely heavy, his mind a little sluggish, nerves a little shattered, but he knew this would be the final push to get to safety and, more importantly, a chance to reach Debbie. Whether that be at her apartment or Parliament Hill, it didn't matter, just as long as she was fine. He knew rest was possibly only a couple more hours away.

During the night he had considered his plan to head over to Debbie's flat in detail, imagining himself climbing the stairs to her flat, banging on the door, his heart racing, wondering if she would be there. He imagined she wouldn't answer, not be there or worse, and he would probably kick the door in, but what would be waiting on the other side? Yes, the thought had returned, the one he had so desperately tried to avoid, so desperate to think of reasons as to how they could have survived. But the more tired he became, the more overwhelming those negative thoughts were.

Then, during the early hours Ron had approached him, carrying cans of Cola he had found in one of the offices. He had offered one to John, who gratefully accepted, and both had silently drunk it while staring into the darkened night. Ron finally broke the silence by offering to take over, but John refused, determined to stay alert until it was all over.

He had decided to tell Ron his plan, saying he was more than welcome to drop him off and then get the others to safety, not wanting to take any more risks.

But Ron had his own plans which he had been thinking about, and they had kept him awake. He told John how he intended to check up on his daughter, just in case she was there, and both shared a smile of admiration, knowing both would do what they intended to.

'How about us dropping by Debbie's flat and then calling at your daughter's place?' John had suggested, wanting to keep the band together, but wanting to do his visit first.

Ron smiled. 'Sure.'

He was glad the policeman would back him up. John was a hero in his eyes, and was doing the police force proud. Also, he was dreading going on alone.

Ron had thanked him again for what he had done, glanced from John to Keith, who was still cradling his dead wife. He had wanted to say something comforting, but knew he would be wasting his time, so without another word he left.

Mary, Mathew and Ron stood together, while Jake and Emma stood opposite; as for Keith, he remained on the floor, holding on to Margaret's body, ignoring the words spoken to him, just clutching his shattered world. Slumped in defeat, he had remained there all night long, not once going to sleep and not once speaking to John, who had stood not far from him. John had glanced at Keith occasionally and thought about saying something, but he knew he would have been wasting his time. He had been in this situation before, too many times unfortunately, having to try and comfort relatives of murdered victims, families having lost other members of the family in house fires. He knew how despair affected people and was sure only professional help could help Keith.

'Suppose we had better make a move soon,' John said. He glanced at Ron and said, 'We shall scout for a vehicle if you like, see what we can find.' Then he looked at the others and said, 'And please, the rest of you remain here.'

John stared at them all a little while longer, hoping they were taking him seriously. He didn't fancy trying to chase after Mary again, he just didn't have the energy.

He stepped outside, waiting for Ron.

Ron turned to Mary and said, 'Try talking to him, see if he wishes to carry on, but if he wishes to remain here then that's his choice, we can't stop him, can't make him join us. We will just have to send help to him, once we find it.'

Mary gave a nod.

Ron placed his hand on her shoulder and told her they would be back as soon as possible, but before leaving he advised her that if anything should happen, she must head upstairs and lock her and Mathew in one of the offices.

She again nodded, grasped his arm and said, 'Ron, thanks for everything you have done for us, and be careful, eh?'

He smiled, and then glanced at Jake.

'Do keep an eye on everybody, eh?'

Jake didn't reply and just stared Ron out. Then he glanced at Keith, knowing it was going to be risky relying on him, what with his head all fucked up. Then he looked at Mary and her son, knowing they had already got them into trouble, and with the pisshead having the hots for her, his balls leading over reason, he could easily jeopardise all of their lives if a situation like this should arise again, and he was so sure it would. So Jake was confident they would be better off without them all.

And right there and then was the ideal time for him to launch his plan, especially now those two eagle-eyed bastards were out of the way, and he was sure it was only a matter of hours, a day tops, before things started to get back to normal. Back to struggling on the streets, unless they acted soon.

He glanced at Emma and beckoned her to join him away from the others. She did, but hesitantly.

'Listen, you have always said I was a great dreamer, but never one to make a move when it came to reality… Well, this may sound ludicrous, but I believe it's the plan I have been waiting all my life to put into action,' Jake said.

Then he told her his plan, the plan he had been working on all night long, giving as much detail as he could, hoping to entice her, so she would give him the courage he needed.

He smiled and added, 'And I know I have said it before, but I believe this is the one; it would give me a chance to put things right between us…'

Emma shook her head at the madness of it all, it just sounded like another dream of his, but then she considered what she had been doing to keep them going, and if he could pull it off, it would be a chance to actually get on in the world, without having to go running back to her parents. The very thought of having to tell them they were right was so heartbreaking and humiliating, and for once she would have to sit back and let him take control, just like she had been hoping he would. And she was intrigued to know how he would cope, and if he didn't and fouled up like before, she could always say goodbye, finally swallow her pride.

She smiled as she realised she was finally in a position to watch him perform, and if he failed, she knew what she had to do.

'Well?' he asked.

She smiled, knowing this was his final chance.

'Let's go, eh?' Jake said, a smile stretching across his face, enjoying his moment of being idolised, Emma giving him the look he loved, worth the many disappointments.

She glanced at the others and for a moment or two wondered if she was doing the right thing. Not wanting to leave them, her caring instinct coming through, but then again she was sure that life was about survival and they had got through some tough times. She was sure the people they had known during this crisis would be more than happy to see the back of them once they reached safety; she had seen it in their eyes.

'Well?' he asked again.

She nodded, determined to give him the benefit of the doubt.

Then, without hesitation, he led her out of the building and into the city, yelling, 'LONDON, MY LONDON.'

Mary had watched them leave and kind of expected it. She glanced at Keith, who shrieked, 'THAT'S IT, YOU GO AND LOOK AFTER YOURSELVES. DON'T YOU CARE ABOUT ME.'

They were the first words he had spoken since Margaret died. He began to cry again, rocking his dead wife in his arms, sobbing aloud.

Mary just pulled Mathew close, petrified by Keith's pain and anguish. She had been planning to try and speak to him, but just couldn't pluck up the courage, just couldn't.

Minutes later, John and Ron reappeared, and Mathew offered them both a huge smile, with Ron returning a wink.

Mary told them about Jake and Emma's departure, and while John and Ron listened, they both failed to look shocked; they had seen their sort before, John having arrested plenty. Both were shocked they had stuck with them for so long and felt sure they knew what they would do, the only thing they knew how to do; those sort never change.

'We managed to find a black cab,' Ron said, recalling finding it outside Euston station, the cab driver slumped over the wheel.

They had had to release the dead man's grip, and lay his body on the floor next to a woman and child. So heartbreaking for the both of them.

'Why don't you take them to the car?' John said, glancing at Ron. Then he looked at Keith, knowing he had one last thing to do.

Ron led Mary and Mathew to the cab while John went over to Keith. He placed his hand on his shoulder and asked him if he wanted to join them.

Keith looked into John's eyes and shook his head.

John patted him on his shoulder, having expected the answer, and then gave him the gun, told him there were two or three bullets left if any of those things returned, and told him the safety catch was off so it was ready to use. Then he told him he would send for help once they reached safety.

Keith thanked him for the gun, holding on to something he had protested against all his life, and yet there and then it felt like his best friend, his answer. He watched John leave. He stared at the gun again, feeling calm and sure.

John got into the cab, glanced at Ron and indicated with a nod for him to drive. As they pulled away, they heard a shot.

Ron, Mary and Mathew glanced round, but not John. He had seen the look in Keith's eyes, a look of torment and self-hate.

It was the only way.

The only way.

30

Day 3

LOWER HOLLOWAY

8.12 a.m.

They had been parked outside a block of flats for ten minutes, the engine still ticking, this being the only noise. All four were staring at the three-storey building, the one John had said Debbie lived in. Debbie's flat, on the top floor to the right, had the blinds drawn, and just like every other flat and house nearby, there seemed to be no signs of life. John imagined and hoped they had all been evacuated, noticing signs on lamp posts that had been placed there recently and were reassuring, warning of potential looters, and stating that burglary was a criminal offence, and that there were CCTVs.

'Would you like me to come with you, mate?' Ron asked, breaking the silence.

John glanced at Ron and shook his head.

He looked at Mary and Mathew and said, 'Just stay in the car, whatever happens, and make sure the doors are locked.'

John looked back to Ron and said, 'Remember, any signs of trouble, just drive away.'

'Just be careful, eh?' Ron said, offering the officer his baton, which John gratefully accepted.

John gave a slight nod and offered them all a smile. He had a feeling they wouldn't leave him and was touched by the thought.

He got out of the taxi and just for a moment glanced around, the silence so unreal, almost frightening. He noticed bloodstains, and imagined the police together with the army had been removing bodies. He stared at the apartment block again, feeling a little giddy, recalling the mayhem they had witnessed, the crazed flashing through his mind, the murdered and those being murdered, there to haunt him forever.

He decided to have a cigarette before going in, just to calm him a little, brace himself for whatever he may see, as he had been imagining the worst while he was in the car, imagining his Debbie dead along with Fiona.

He took a deep breath, determined to make his move, dropped the half-smoked cigarette and crushed it underfoot, muttering to himself, 'To hell with it.'

He stood for a short while in front of the flat door, recalling yet again the horrors in his mind of what he was expecting to find upon entering. If he found her dead, he knew it would destroy him, but then again, perhaps she was injured, or had gone to Parliament Hill.

He knocked just the once and felt dread. When there was no reply, he banged again and again, almost becoming frantic. He thought about kicking the door in, but instead grabbed the handle and to his surprise the door opened.

After taking a deep breath to try to calm himself down, the way he would before any anxious moment, he crossed the threshold, expecting to see it trashed or even worse. But instead, he was greeted with a half-empty room, most of the expensive items gone.

Bastards! he thought, thinking of the looters. He rushed through each room, not wanting to waste too much time thinking, wanting to see if his Debbie was there. But she wasn't, though he noticed some essential items were also missing.

John headed back to the living room, relieved to not have witnessed what he had been dreading, and his head cleared and the trembling stopped. He noticed an envelope where the television used to be.

He picked it up, noticing his name was written on it, and he smiled as he eagerly tore it open.

John,

I guessed you would come here to check up on us at some stage, the great bloke that you are... Well, thanks for doing so, and as you have noticed most of our belongings have gone. We have moved them into Justin's strongroom, and we, along with Justin, have gone to Parliament Hill, as we were advised. And, John, I do hope you're fine, as I know you must have seen it really bad with what went down. You're in my prayers. Hope to see you there soon. Xxx Debbie.

John smiled, so relieved she was okay. He felt choked by her letter, but after reading it again he felt deflated. Justin was looking after them when that was John's job. Yes, good old Justin was there for Debbie when it came to organisation as well, then proving to be the macho man by getting them to safety, offering her security, proving to be more of a man than he had given him credit for.

He thought about the others waiting for him in the car, people he had known for less than forty-eight hours, and yet they had shown him more compassion and loyalty than Debbie and her friends had ever done. He imagined that Debbie, Fiona and Justin were laughing and joking, poor old John truly out of sight and out of mind. And after all the worrying he had done.

He reflected how he would go to pieces when he was around Debbie, because of the way she made him feel.

He screwed up the letter in his hand, sighed and then headed for the door, wondering how she would react when she saw him.

How would he react?

But he knew how, and it was that thought which frustrated him.

31

Day 3

EUSTON STREET

8.15 a.m.

'So where are we heading?' Emma asked as they turned onto Euston Street, though in the back of her mind she was sure she already knew, as she had been that way before, with a client.

She hoped he wasn't heading there, and told herself to calm down; he wouldn't be that crazy. Then she occupied her thoughts by focusing on the carnage along Euston Street, trying to adjust to it, but it still looked intimidating, frightening and upsetting. But not to Jake, who seemed focused, unfazed by it all, buzzing on his plans, as if the human corpses were there just to be kicked at or possibly robbed; he had already gone through a suited man and woman's pockets as they lay near a shop, smiling when he managed to steal forty pounds from them and a packet of cigarettes.

'We are heading for Eddie's flat, and all being well, he won't be there. Then of course it will be a free for all,' Jake said, offering her a huge smile, pulling her close, strolling along Euston Street as if he didn't have a care in the world.

Suddenly, he was kicking another body and cheering away as if he had scored a winning goal for England. For the first time in his life he was finally going to make a right move, and felt for sure that he was born for this moment. He felt so proud of himself. He offered Emma a cigarette from the packet he had just stolen, which she accepted, though a little hesitantly at first.

Emma had begun to question her sanity, as it seemed to her that yet again, Jake was not taking himself seriously, not taking the situation seriously, because if anything were to go wrong, where would they run to? And who might they run into? When it came to heroes and villains, she knew where Jake stood; she wondered again, would he use her as bait while he fled?

'Trust me, just this once, everything is going to work out just fine,' Jake said, hoping to take away the doubt in her eyes, but knew only his actions would be able to do that. He was going to prove to her that he could do it, make her so proud of him. He then nudged her playfully and said, 'Just imagine, a few years from now they will be making a movie about all this, may even want to use real actors who had been through it like us. They might want to use our story as well, just imagine that. I think I would settle for, let's say, one hundred K.'

Emma began to laugh. Jake smiled, proud he could lift her spirits even in their current situation, and while they made the short journey to Eddie's flat he told her again about what he intended to do, but in more detail, to try and erase the doubt she was feeling. And rather than her thinking it was all talk, she would hopefully then have a little faith in him, and realise they could actually land on their feet for a change.

'What do we do if he's there?' Emma asked, doubt creeping into her mind, wondering if it was going to be another blunder.

She knew the sort of person Eddie was and knew how he hated Jake, having told her so on many occasions after they had had sex. Therefore, she knew it was probably going to be another fight or flight scenario, and every time it was flight, she needed seriously convincing. Jake was too calm and playful for her to be to convinced, though; it was as if it was all a game to him and she feared what Eddie might do to them.

'We tell him we were checking up on him, seeing if he is alright, looking for a place to hide,' Jake said, knowing Eddie was paranoid, but also what he would do the moment he answered the door; if he was still around.

Jake wasn't going to give him a chance to pull off anything defensive though, and would use the iron bar if he had to. He wouldn't have to work up the aggression, as he seriously hated him, and he would prove to himself he had it in him to harm someone when he had to. He would bash his head in, in no time at all, as he had often seen how he looked at Emma, how he whispered to her and craved to be with her. He had often imagined she had slept with him; perhaps he was a regular punter. So he would pound the bar on his skull, just as Eddie would pound his Emma in bed, and he wouldn't stop until his head cracked wide open, spilling out his shit for brains.

'Wait here, eh, while I go and see if he's in,' Jake said as they entered the stairwell.

'Just be careful,' Emma told him, believing this was just another ludicrous idea, destined to fail, wishing she had stayed with the others.

She had always longed for him to make a decision, and it seemed he had briefly thought things through, but she never thought he would try and rob the likes of Eddie.

He kissed her on the lips and nodded.

'I'll be careful, promise. And trust me, things will work out.'

Jake dropped the half-smoked cigarette and crushed it.

Emma looked into his deep-blue eyes and wanted to believe him so much, wanted desperately for his plan to work. She had longed for many of his plans to work, and it had pained her when they hadn't. She then found herself slipping into thoughts of Eddie, feeling a sadness and warmth towards him.

Jake banged on the flat door three or four times, clutching the iron bar, telling himself he could do this.

He knew there was no way Eddie would leave town, not with what he had to hide.

Then again, when the incident happened he would have more than likely been on his rounds. And if that was the case, then no doubt he would have met his end, as he would have panicked, and either got himself killed by some of those crazed or smashed up his car.

And Jake had convinced himself that was the truth. But still, he had to be prepared, just in case.

And when there was no reply, he grinned and then began kicking the front door, cursing with each kick until it finally burst open. He rushed in, to be greeted by an empty flat.

He allowed himself to laugh; point proven. He went over to the stairs and shouted to Emma to join him.

They managed to find a small stash of drugs, but whatever he had in large quantities must be locked in the safe hidden in the bedroom; however, it was easy enough for Emma to find.

'Well, it's a start,' Jake said, ripping into the bag and firing some of the drugs down his throat.

Emma did the same, and they both laughed, collapsing on Eddie's bed, wrestling and playing around, then relaxing side by side for a little while. Both stared blindly at the ceiling, enjoying the sensation of being high at Eddie's expense, feeling relaxed and content. Nothing in the world mattered, everything that had happened seeming like nothing more than a dream.

Emma broke the silence by asking what his next plan was, feeling so proud of her man.

'Our next stop is Leroy's; he is loaded with gear,' Jake said, getting to his feet, feeling the best he had for God knows how long.

He let out a scream of delight, and Emma joined him.

Emma got to her feet, placed the small bag of drugs in her pocket and glanced at the safe.

'Pity we don't know his combination.'

Jake stared at it, knowing Eddie did well when it came to shifting gear, and that there would no doubt be at least three or four thousand pounds in cash in there, as well as the top notch drugs he sold in Soho, and even Chelsea way.

'Well, suppose we could always have a bash at breaking the code,' Jake said, smiling, a wicked glint in his eye. 'Not like anyone is going to come around and stop us, is it?'

'But what if he comes back? I mean, he is bound to sooner or later,' Emma said.

Jake laughed. 'He won't be coming back.'

They tried half a dozen different combinations, writing down each one, feeling frustrated for getting it wrong.

'It has to be something simple, something a dummy like him wouldn't forget,' Jake said, trying to consider what it might be, sitting next to Emma.

Emma smiled as a possibility came to mind. She tried one combination, and then on the second attempt it opened.

Jake kissed her on her lips and asked how she had worked it out.

'The day he was born, the flat number and his lucky number he often mentioned; just wasn't sure which order it would be in,' she said, feeling proud of herself and accepting another kiss off Jake.

And how did she know all this? Jake thought, feeling stung.

His suspicions now seemed like real possibilities; but their gains were more important to him right now.

There was about five thousand in the safe and four packets of cocaine, as well as a small quantity of heroin and other drugs.

They hugged each other. Finally, after so much struggling, it looked as if they were going to come out on top, something positive to be gained from so much carnage.

'So, do remind me of our plan, Mr Clever Clogs?' Emma said as she helped him put the money and drugs in a carrier bag they had found.

'As I said, we hit Leroy's, which will definitely be an open invitation, as he would have been doing his rounds around King's Cross when this thing happened. And believe me, that guy is minted. Then we'll hit a few more I know of.' He hugged the bag they had just filled and said, 'First, though, our next move is to steal a car, do the raids, hide our gains for a little while, dump the car and then in time, it's farewell to London and hello to possibly Manchester, our new base ... our new life.'

Emma smiled at his plan, happy they were finally on the up; it made everything they had been through seem worthwhile.

They exited the flat together and, while Emma waited near the entrance, clutching their gains, Jake hunted around the cars that were nearby, finally deciding on a hatchback; it was a little dated, but sporty, one that he had always dreamed of owning. Its windows had been smashed, but everything else looked fine. He brushed the glass from the seat, jumped in and began hot-wiring, something he wasn't very good at and had only done once or twice; the tabs he had taken weren't helping either.

Then suddenly, he heard footsteps.

'Not the policeman and that fucking tube worker,' he said, sitting up, ready to thump them, but it wasn't them; it was three or four of those crazed people heading in his direction, pounding the concrete to get at him, like a bunch of savages, wanting to tear him to shreds.

He shut himself in the car, but knew it was pointless, as there were no windows. He cursed them, wondering where the hell they had come from, cursed himself for not noticing them, the excitement and drugs overshadowing caution. Bastard!

He then began fumbling with the wires, desperately trying to start the car; luckily it started. He slammed it into reverse and headed for Emma, the car bouncing a few times as it went over bodies. Upon reaching Emma, he pushed the passenger door open, trying his best to brush away the glass from the seat, and ordered her in. But she just stood there, staring at those crazed things, which were getting closer and closer, remembering how they had attacked Lisa and Margaret, the sadness overwhelming her.

He leaned across, grabbed the bag from her and ordered her again to get in, but she was too upset and petrified to move, and those crazed things were getting closer and closer, so without a moment to lose he slammed his foot against the accelerator and jetted forward, cursing her for ignoring him. He stared in the rear-view mirror at Emma, who just continued to stare, the pain of her knowing that combination still stinging, her hesitation about going into Eddie's flat a little painful, convincing himself he was doing the right thing. Staring a little longer than he should, he did not see what he was heading towards.

Emma was suddenly shaken out of the spell by a loud bang as the car Jake was driving smashed into a lamp post. Then, a breath of air later, the car burst into flames, Jake screaming as he tried to get out.

Emma became aware of the crazed people heading her way, so she turned and headed back to the flat, covering her ears, not wanting to listen to the burning of the car, Jake's screams, not wanting to accept what was happening.

She slammed the flat door shut and pushed the settee against it, knowing it wasn't going to be enough to hold them off. She could hear their footsteps on the stairs as she relived the horror of what she had just seen, Jake's screams still ripping through her mind, terrifying her. She headed into the bedroom, pushed as much furniture against the door as she could, knowing once again they would soon get in.

She cried, wishing she had stayed with the others; although that was bound to have ended in disaster too.

She collapsed in a heap, her dad's words returning to haunt her. Then she pulled out the small bag of drugs, knowing there were two ways she could die, the drugs being the best option. She started muttering for her parents' forgiveness.

32

Day 3

HACKNEY

8.47 a.m.

'So, what do you think your daughter would have decided to do?' John asked, breaking the silence that had fallen between them since he'd returned from Debbie's flat.

He had told them Debbie was probably at Parliament Hill, ignoring the kind words and remaining silent during the journey to Hackney, not wanting the conversation to be on his situation. Mary, Mathew and Ron also remained silent, wondering what they might discover.

'With a bit of luck she would have gone to the rescue centre, but you just never know ... she can be unpredictable,' Ron said, wanting to say something light-hearted, to glorify his daughter a little, but he couldn't, as he was thinking again about the bunch of wasters she called friends.

He so hated them and would be surprised if they had a brain cell between them. He imagined they had probably panicked when the explosion happened, all looking out for number one, wanting to scramble out of that place as fast as they could, no concern for anyone else; but not Libby, she would be far too worried about the others to look out for herself, putting those lowlifes first.

Ron glanced at John and said, 'Thanks for sticking with me on this one.'

John smiled, feeling proud of himself.

Ron stared at the house Libby called home. It was on a quiet suburban street, neighbours' cars still parked outside the houses; it looked as if the area hadn't been hit all that bad, though there were police notices on the lamp posts just like over in Lower Holloway. Most of the other houses seemed welcoming, with flowers in the window or something else homely; not Libby's house, though. No, there was grubby lace hanging from the windows, windows that hadn't been cleaned in years, the front door battered and in need of a lick of paint. Ron felt so ashamed of the place Libby had called home. So ashamed to bring the people he hardly knew here, as if it was his fault she was living there; he felt like he had failed her so badly.

He got out of the car without saying a word or making eye contact and climbed the steps. He tried the door, but it was locked, so he knocked and carried on knocking for a short while. When there was no reply, he imagined they were out and dreaded the thought that they could be looting. He scouted around, knowing they were bound to have a spare key hiding somewhere, as they were often out of their faces. He found it under the doormat and wished they could have thought of a better place. He unlocked the door, the first time he had ever entered Libby's domain, and it hurt him to think she had not once invited him over.

Inside, the carpet stuck to his feet and there was a stale stench of urine. The floor was cluttered with junk, food cartons and empty beer cans, and the walls were covered in torn wallpaper. As he focused on the so-called living quarters, he was shocked, although he had kind of expected it.

There was a mattress on the floor, syringes at the side.

He turned to leave, not wanting to be in the house any longer, feeling disgusted with himself and his daughter; he had failed his daughter again.

John, Mary and Mathew all expected him to say something when he returned, but he didn't; he just got in the car and sat there, staring blindly out of the window, so John, who had taken over as driver, started the engine.

As he drove away, he said, 'Would you like to check on your house?'

Mary recalled the bloodbath back there and the possibility the crazed could be waiting for them, but so could Jamie, so she told him where they lived in East Finchley. It was quite a journey from where they were, possibly half an hour's drive. She sat back and hoped and prayed they wouldn't meet any of those crazed things or, worse, find Jamie dead.

John stood with Mathew on the drive while Ron entered the house with Mary, John noticing blood on the neighbours' drive yet no sign of bodies; perhaps the army had been there already and removed them. He wondered where they would store them all, and about the funeral arrangements. He imagined there would be a week of mourning.

John suddenly felt depressed and needed to change his thoughts, so he placed his hand on Mathew's shoulder and said, 'How about if we join your mum?'

Mathew nodded and led the way.

Mary was standing in the reception room, with Ron a few steps behind her. What used to be a well-organised room, everything having its rightful place, was now a complete shambles; even the curtains and lace that hung from the huge bow windows had been torn down.

John stood just in front of Mathew.

'Mum?' Mathew said, wondering what had happened, why they had been targeted.

Suddenly, before Mary could reply, there was a bump, shortly followed by another, coming from the room above.

'Dad?' Mathew said.

But Mary didn't look convinced. She held on to Mathew and glanced at Ron and John.

'You two wait here,' John said to them. He glanced at Ron and said, 'If you wait at the bottom of the stairs, I'll go and see what's going on.'

Ron shook his head. 'No, mate, I'll be following.'

John didn't argue, and smiled.

He had his baton and CS spray ready, knowing, though, that if it was the crazed up there they wouldn't be able to stop them, but all the same, it gave him a little reassurance.

He crept up the open-plan staircase, Ron close behind, both listening hard, visions of the endless and mindless crazed returning thick and fast. Finally, they paused as they reached the top, and noticed that the shuffling and bumping had stopped, as if whoever it was had sensed them, knew they were there, waiting to make their move.

John glanced at Ron and signalled for him to wait where he was. Then he took the final step so he was up on the landing, convinced it was looters.

There in front of him was the master bedroom, to his right another bedroom and behind it the bathroom. He glanced in the direction of the master bedroom again, noticing the door was ajar. He tightened his grip on his weapons and then kicked open the door, pouncing into the room. A second later, the mist cleared and he saw that the room had been ransacked, but no obvious signs of looters, as most of the valuables were scattered on the floor. It was as if somebody had just gone crazy in there.

He turned to see Ron behind him, and before either could speak and give their thoughts on what might have happened there, they heard a loud bang from down the hallway. They immediately vacated the room to see a crazed man with another two in tow racing towards them.

John pushed Ron towards the stairs and told him to run, both racing down them like mad, almost slipping, with the sound of the crazed not far behind, almost feeling their breath on their necks.

They rushed into the reception room and slammed the door shut, throwing their entire weight against it. Mary and Mathew just stared, stunned by what they were seeing.

'Mary, head for the car and start it up!' John ordered, the door beginning to vibrate, the force of the crazed trying to get at them, the beasts the other side growling and groaning.

Without hesitation she rushed outside and leapt into the cab, Mathew at her side. Seconds later, John and Ron came rushing out of the house and dived through the open car doors, and a split second later there was the screeching of tyres as the car jetted away, all four of them not wanting to look back, all eager to get to safety.

Parliament Hill bound.

33

Day 3

PARLIAMENT HILL BOUND

9.51 a.m.

It took a while before their breathing slowed and their heads cleared. Once they could think clearly again, they were left wondering what they were going to find, not sure if there would be a happy ending to it all, possibilities racing through their minds of worst-case scenarios and desperate to work out how they would survive if those scenarios were to become reality. What if the camp had been taken over by those things, just like one of those horrid zombie films? They imagined they could be heading from one disaster to another, and would have to keep on moving, just like a Mad Max film, until desperation set in. But then what? Might they turn on each other, or would they just give up the way Keith had?

John broke the silence by advising Mary to follow the signs along Highgate West Hill, directing them to the entrance to Parliament Hill. Upon approaching, they noticed thousands of cars parked along the road, on drives, grass verges, anywhere and everywhere. John imagined the camp being overpopulated, since there were far too many people in the London suburb to fit on Parliament Hill.

Mathew pointed in the direction of Parliament Hill, as he could see caravans, thousands of them, all gleaming in the sun.

'Looks like things are going to be fine,' Ron said, offering Mathew a smile.

They then turned onto Millfield Lane and crossed the High Gate Ponds, with cameras following their every move. They all sighed in relief when they saw armed police behind a barricade in the road, in front of a constructed sheet fence that stretched as far as the eye could see. The officers all wore gas masks, and one of the police officers signalled them to stop, which they did. They glanced at each other and allowed themselves to laugh out loud, all so relieved it was finally over, wanting to jump out of the car and hug the police.

Then in a flash they became reflective again, remembering the people they had met and who had unfortunately died along the way, and the carnage they had witnessed. They wondered what had happened to Jake and Emma, but were sure they had survived, as somehow those sort always seem to come out on top. They relived the terror they had felt, the emotional journey, finding it hard not to shed a tear.

Men wearing white outfits and breathing aspirators appeared through an opening in the sheet fence and asked them all to get out of the car. They were led through the barricade and then the entrance through which the men had appeared, straight into a quarantine area filled with white tents and tunnels. They were greeted by more people dressed in white, and for as far as the eye could see, everything was bleached white, the personal and the surroundings becoming one mass of whiteness, distinguished only by the words people spoke. But it was all medical jargon, nothing they could understand.

They were taken into separate compartments where they had to strip, be showered and medically examined, then dressed in jumpsuits. They were then individually led to a cabin, which was a makeshift interview room, where a panel of three people sat behind a desk, all wearing suits, a woman in the far corner taking notes. They were asked their names, next of kin and details, where they had been and so on, and then they were taken back to the medical rooms where further examinations were carried out, poked and prodded like a piece of meat. Finally, they were taken to waiting transport and went on a short drive to a cabin, surrounded by caravans, with people everywhere, all wearing gas masks; a miniature civilisation covering almost the entire 932 acres. Even most of the trees had been chopped down to make room, which was a crime as far as they were concerned. There was a huge armed presence, reminding them it wasn't over yet, though the sun shone on the vans, making them gleam and shine like stars; a welcome sight. They also noticed the green mist had practically gone.

Since they arrived, John, Mary and Ron had constantly been asking if anyone had seen or heard from their next of kin, but no one gave them a straight answer, and they realised the attitude of authorities hadn't changed.

They were then asked to go into the cabin and take a seat; then finally, they were left alone. They removed the breathing aspirators, feeling rough, tired, hungry and emotional. Mathew was the only one doing the talking, and while he talked, the others sat in silence, reflecting once again on what they had been through, all feeling the warm sun on their faces as it streamed through a window; it was the first time in what seemed like a lifetime that they had noticed such pleasures.

Ron glanced at John and said, 'Do you know one of the first things I'm going to do when all this gets back to normal again?'

John shook his head, his mind still fuzzy.

'Buy myself a new motorbike, a real devil, and have a right blast,' Ron said, thinking of his love. 'One that I had always promised myself and never bought.'

John grinned. 'And I shall buy myself a new one and give you a race down to Brighton, if you like?'

'You're on,' Ron said, winking.

Within five minutes, an officer had returned. He stepped aside to allow a tall gentleman to enter, and as he did so, Mary jumped to her feet along with Mathew and rushed over to him.

They hugged each other and cried, saying how much they had missed each other, how much they meant to each other, how much they loved each other, looking forward to having a long heart-to-heart.

John and Ron glanced at each other and smiled, proud of what they had achieved; it made the whole journey seem worthwhile.

They watched them leave and prayed there was good news for them too.

Then, moments later, another officer entered, along with a woman.

'So, you managed to join us,' Debbie said, a smile on her face.

John smiled, got to his feet and hugged her, thinking how happy he was to be with her.

Ron remained seated, glad for them, and watched them leave hand in hand, just like Mary and her husband had, like some old Western film from long ago with a happy ending.

Ron was alone again, just like he had been for many years, other than the short, wonderful spells with his daughter. Even though he recalled Libby's living quarters and how disappointed he had felt, he knew he could never give up on her and he was so looking forward to seeing her again. But the officer didn't return again and no good news came, and as the minutes turned to hours, he felt deflated, alone, totally isolated. He recalled what he would normally do when he was feeling like that; he would have a cigarette, put on some music and possibly have a glass of whisky, but there were none of those pleasures here, apart from the handful of cigarettes he had; he supposed one out of three wasn't too bad. He got to his feet and exited the waiting area. He asked the officer who was in the other room if he had any news for him, but he just shook his head, trying to be as sincere as possible, a routine he had no doubt practised over and over during the past few days.

Ron stood near the exit and lit a cigarette, ignoring the No Smoking sign and the sign stating breathing aspirators must be worn beyond this point. He wondered if this was it for him, and at the same time had a gut feeling it wasn't over yet; nightmares don't have happy endings.

34

Day 3

PARLIAMENT HILL

6.12 p.m.

Ron had been given a small caravan to stay in about three hundred feet up Parliament Hill, overlooking most of the other vans but not quite at the peak, vulnerable to wind, especially since most of the trees had been felled, and he was sure it would rock the van and was bound to keep him awake. Inside it was pokey, a little untidy and had obviously been used before, but that didn't matter to Ron; he had stayed in worse places, roughed it many a time, especially when he had been out on his bike for some weekend away. But the one thing that did annoy him was that there was no alcohol and nowhere to get any either, and therefore sleep was going to be extremely difficult. And it seemed nobody wanted to help; they just looked straight through you and totally ignored you. Nothing had changed about people's attitudes, no pulling together in a crisis, everybody just concerned about themselves. He had found himself wondering if it had been the same during The Blitz, all those black and white footage films showing families working together just for propaganda. Had they been kept in the dark like they were now, led to believe things would be fine? Something else that really annoyed him about the campsite was that smoking wasn't allowed inside the caravans, with very sensitive sprinklers fitted to make sure you didn't. They had certainly put an awful lot of thought into the site in the short time they had to erect it, and he couldn't help but wonder if the government had been expecting what had happened.

And as for the breathing mask he had to wear, what was the point? He couldn't smoke anyway with that stupid thing on, and smoking was all he had left, other than his thoughts of course, and he recalled the interesting meeting he had had to sit through earlier; well, it was more of an interrogation really. He had been sitting in the canteen, just finishing off his meal, when two army soldiers asked him to join them, and led him to a small complex and into a room where three officers sat waiting for him, one an army officer the other two police officers. They wanted to know how he had managed to survive and for him to relive every step of their journey. One of the police officers made notes, and on finishing their discussion they all offered him a brief handshake. But when he tried asking questions, they did not want to reply.

He recalled being told briefly why the communications were down, something to do with a biological weapon that scrambled all forms of transmission – the green gas. But they said they were working on getting things back to normal as soon as possible, and that the camp was a kind of processing centre, out of which most people were being airlifted and taken to other camps.

Ron glanced at his mobile again – they certainly hadn't sorted the problem out yet, and he was looking forward to when his phone would start working again so that he could make those calls he desperately needed to. He started watching people below, something to occupy his mind, occasionally glancing at the overcast sky that was getting darker and enjoying his cigarette. Only three more untouched cigarettes remained and then life was destined to be hell; but surely he would be able to scrounge some from somewhere. He would have to.

Then again, he hadn't met many pleasant people so far, and all he had seen apart from the ignorance was how they were becoming agitated, arguing; no, nothing had changed. The people in the neighbouring vans weren't sociable either, and reminded him of his ex-flat neighbours.

He got to his feet, dropped what remained of his cigarette and crushed it underfoot. Then he glanced around, and saw that the only protection the compound had was a makeshift sheet fence, which was not very reassuring if the crazed should decide to gatecrash. And if they did get in, it would be a slaughterhouse.

He found himself wondering again where his daughter might be, and what had happened to his ex and her partner. No, they weren't very good at providing information here, always stalling, making an excuse as to why they couldn't answer the questions that mattered, leaving you with a sympathetic smile. "As soon as we hear something, we will let you know," which basically meant, don't bother us with your domestics. Heartless, the fucking lot of them.

He shook his head, knowing now why everyone was pissed off, and then headed down the hill, wanting to stretch his legs before calling it a night.

He headed down the hill while holding his mask, but had no intention of wearing it. There were dogs barking, children screaming, people arguing and the scowling eyes of the soldiers. And this was supposed to be safety. Ron thought it was like a time bomb. He studied everything and everyone, observing, the way he did for a living, not participating. That was how he had always lived his life, the only way he knew how to live.

'Eh, man, where you going?' came a voice from behind him.

Ron turned to see a tall, dark soldier who was removing his mask. He looked in his early twenties and seemed a little edgy. Ron recognised his face, but couldn't quite place him, since he had spoken to and seen so many people.

'Just having a walk,' Ron replied, still trying to remember where he had seen him before.

'You're not supposed to leave the restricted area,' the guard said, pointing to a line Ron had crossed.

Ron noticed he had crossed a yellow painted line and for some reason had been heading towards the fence. He recalled someone telling him about the rules and regulations, but like always he had just ignored them, lost interest and got bored.

'So sorry,' he replied with a smile, though deep down he couldn't give a shit.

The soldier frowned and said, 'It's okay, how were you supposed to know? They didn't explain it all that well when you arrived. And no doubt you have had an awful lot on your mind.'

Ron then recalled that he was one of the soldiers who had noted down his details.

'So, how long have you been here?' Ron asked, offering him one of his last three cigarettes.

The soldier gratefully accepted and appreciated Ron lighting it for him.

'I was in Afghanistan when all this broke out and got drafted back here. Rumours were that terrorists had struck and that was what the press were led to believe, but the truth is, there's more to it than that.'

He smiled at Ron, as if wondering whether to tell him what was on his mind, perhaps unsure of Ron's intentions. There was certainly a hell of a lot of paranoia around, and he decided to concentrate on his cigarette instead.

'We shall never know, son, never,' Ron said, easing the soldier's mind, not wanting him to feel pressurised into saying anything. Friendship was never formed through pressurising someone.

'By the way, the name's Dwaine,' the young soldier said. 'And if you don't mind me asking, you seem to have managed to survive out there with your friends for quite some time...'

Ron grinned. It seemed all they were interested in was their story, and he couldn't help but wonder why.

'Well, it's been a pleasure talking to you, Dwaine,' Ron said, briefly shaking his hand before replacing his mask, just to impress.

Then he headed back the way he had come, feeling happy he had made the young man's acquaintance, feeling for sure something positive would come from doing so. He could feel the soldier's eyes burning into his back, and he was convinced he would see him again.

He slowly climbed the hill, the evening maturing into total darkness, making the ground a little slippery.

Caravan lights were lit, the residents taking their frustrations inside. And as Ron made his journey back to his van he found himself wondering how Mary and her son were, and John too, their vans not far from his own. But no doubt he was long out of mind and couldn't blame them, as he would have been the same. He thought about his daughter again and it saddened him, as she was probably still out there somewhere. Then again, the camp wasn't exactly paradise, and he couldn't help wondering if they would have been better off surviving out there, as this was like a prison; told when to eat, what you can and can't do. His daughter would not have liked that, so perhaps she was better off out there. That thought warmed him, and he knew he would be able to rest a little with that in mind.

Ron was woken by the sound of his mobile bleeping and vibrating, and at first he wondered where he was, confused by the noise. He smiled when he noticed it had come to life again and he had received a message, but he did not recognise the mobile number.

'Communication finally up and running again then,' he said to himself, sitting up.

05.33. Dad, just to let you know lost my mob, lol. We at 1st went 2 Parliament Hill, things weren't good there, something very wrong about the place, so we got out, so we headed Brighton bound and we are now safe. Everything is great down here in Brighton, people very welcoming and trusting. Apparently most of the country is fine. Hope to see you down here soon. Going to get a good night's sleep now though.

He immediately text her back, telling her he would find her and that he was fine, how much he missed her and longed to see her again. He felt so relieved, so happy that she was okay, and the whole journey now seemed worthwhile.

He thought for a moment about the situation he was in, stuck in a flimsy van in the middle of caravan city, their only protection being a flimsy fence. Then there was the cagey attitude of the soldiers. Yes, Libby was right, there was something not right and unhealthy about the place, and one way or another he was going to find out what it was and then get out of there.

35

Day 4

PARLIAMENT HILL

8.49 a.m.

'Any luck with your daughter?' John asked, appearing at the side of Ron, wanting to occupy his mind with thoughts other than those that were driving him mad.

Ron was so tempted to tell him what his daughter had said in her text message, but his mind was on her welfare. He had tried calling her on many occasions, but she had failed to answer and hadn't replied to the texts he had sent, and he had gone through the possible reasons. Perhaps she had taken some of the drugs she had become fond of and was spaced out, or perhaps she was sleeping, a deep sleep. He had considered other things too, but they weren't positive thoughts, and he hoped she would call him at any moment. So to try and lift his spirits a little, he had texted other friends of his, friends he sometimes went drinking with, most of them replying, asking how he was, all stating how mad it had been. He had even heard from a friend of his ex-wife's, saying they all were fine, and he was glad.

'I don't know what you think, but I feel uneasy about this place,' John said.

They stared into the canteen, which had at least two or three hundred diners. John was sure the uneasiness had worsened since all forms of communication had returned. They had heard people talking about videos that had been uploaded onto YouTube showing some of the devastation, news reports stating there had been a terrorist attack in London, the borough of Middlesex and parts of Kent and Surrey being sealed off, nobody allowed to enter, and those that were within the boroughs being asked to head for rescue centres. Conspiracy after conspiracy was heard, and they were told that rogue members of the government were involved, stories going round and round, causing panic. He had even heard that graphic videos had been uploaded to a website which claimed to reveal the truth. A fellow officer had shown him two of the videos, one being of three crazed women attacking a school teacher, cutting her to shreds in front of a bus filled with secondary school children returning from an outing. What sick bastard had filmed that and uploaded it? The other video showed a crazed man, about seventy years old, on the ground while three hooded lads kicked him to a bloody pulp, laughing, and the person recording it kept saying, 'Chavs fight back.' It saddened John, and he knew there was one big mess to clean up. But he had his hands full with one particular lady at the moment.

'So how's your Debbie?' Ron asked, glad he wasn't the only one feeling unnerved by the experience. He thought he would ask to see if John wanted to talk, get whatever was bothering him off his chest, as he sensed there was something on his mind regarding his love life.

John shrugged and pulled a face expressing his uncertainty.

'We are sharing a van with her mate; pair of them are inseparable. Fiona wasn't interested in what we had been through, just went on and on about Justin and her and how they had made this amazing escape. And going on about some fancy man she had been seeing and how he was also here at the camp, poor sod. And now the phones are working they are calling family and friends and so on, so here I am, escaped for a short while.'

Ron nodded and then concentrated on the cigarette John had given him, one of half a dozen, John having used his police authority to scrounge some off the other authorities.

John smiled and said, 'Found out this Justin has a girlfriend; he's with her in his van, and it deflated them a little.'

Yes, the disappointment had been evident in Debbie's eyes, but not as much as Fiona. And as for the previous evening, he had to listen to Fiona banging on about how she thought one of the officers had taken a fancy to her, Debbie once again entranced by her stories, giving her full attention. As for John, he had felt like striking Fiona and then shaking Debbie for listening to such nonsense. It had been one hell of a long evening. But luckily he had needed sleep and so had retired early. He had slept most of the night, but his dreams had been graphic and laced with terror, visions of the dead returning to haunt him, the ones he had killed returning to haunt him, whispering in his ear, asking why he had shot them, Margaret screaming at him not to give Keith the gun. If it hadn't been for the sedatives he was given, no doubt he would have been awake for most of the night.

He smiled as he recalled lying there that morning with Debbie resting her head on his chest, pride and love rising in his throat. He had woken her and told her how much he loved her, and Debbie had declared her love for him. They had made love and then lain side by side in total peace. Though that peace didn't last long as Fiona was banging on the door and then burst in, telling them the mobiles were now working. Debbie had rushed to join her in the living quarters, leaving John alone.

'Listen, mate, when you said there was an uneasy feeling about the place, I think you're right, and I think it's serious...'

'Serious?' John interrupted, wondering what was on Ron's mind, what he had heard.

'I was talking to a guard last night, and he was a little edgy.' Ron decided to tell him about what Libby had said in her text. And when John did not reply straight away, he added, 'Listen, I don't expect you to believe me, but what if I get some hard evidence?'

John burst out laughing, then stopped himself and said, 'Sorry, mate, I didn't mean that to happen, but it all sounds crazy. I mean, hard evidence for what exactly?'

'Evidence that things ain't what they appear to be,' Ron said, feeling a little scolded by his outburst, recalling painful memories of his mates calling him boring snoring Ron behind his back.

John placed his hand on Ron's shoulder and said, 'Listen, mate, just be careful, because believe me, they don't appreciate sceptics. I'd advise you to keep your head down, and before you know it things will be back to normal again, possibly in the next few days.'

'Yes, you're probably right, I guess I'm just overreacting,' Ron said, trying his hardest to sound convinced and to hide the pain he was feeling following the policeman's doubt.

Deep down he was wondering if he could trust John either. It seemed he had been getting close to the authorities, but then he was one of them, and don't all authorities stick together?

They departed with a brief smile and promised to meet up again. Ron decided to head to the far side of the camp, have a snoop around and try to discover some conspiracy to prove John wrong, still feeling hurt by his outburst. Then again, it seemed to him as if the policeman was just obsessed with that poor woman, who was obviously frightened of him, and he was far too busy thinking about her to see what was happening around him. Ron noticed the guards were watching him, as if they sensed he was up to something. On reaching the far end, near a small group of trees, he saw two huge buildings that had recently been erected, like cattle sheds, with all the windows boarded up. He had the urge to head over to them and see what was inside, as he was sure they weren't for storing food. And he realised he was standing in a blind spot so that the guards in the camp wouldn't see.

Suddenly, he felt a hand on his shoulder.

He raised his hands and slowly turned, expecting to be staring into the barrel of a soldier's gun, expecting to be in serious trouble for his lack of respect, but instead, he saw a startled Dwaine, the young soldier he had met previously.

'What the hell is going on in there?' Ron asked, feeling annoyed by all the secrecy.

Dwaine indicated for Ron to follow him with a nod of his head. He led him back towards the camp and then said, 'There is some serious shit going down, and in those warehouses there are dozens if not hundreds of those crazed people.'

'But what on earth are they doing with them all?' Ron asked, dreading the answer.

'They are taking samples and testing them on the normal people here, trying to find the cause and a cure, meddling with nature, as always. But you mustn't tell anyone I have told you this,' Dwaine said, looking scared to death.

Ron offered him a cigarette. 'Listen, son, we have to get out of here. Are you with us?'

'Us?' Dwaine said, frowning.

'There may be a handful more,' Ron said, thinking about John and Mary, and their friends and relatives.

'I have been thinking about it for a while, but if we do go, we can't take too many,' Dwaine said, looking around to make sure nobody had noticed them talking.

'That's fine, and the sooner we get out the better, I reckon,' Ron said, thinking about his Libby, the endless stories circulating; it would only be a matter of time before somebody made the break.

'We'll meet at your van at eight tonight for a quick briefing and then go at eleven, okay?' Dwaine said, starting to walk away.

'Seems pretty soon,' Ron said, thinking perhaps it would be better to wait until the following day, to give him enough time to convince the others.

'Listen, we have to go tonight,' Dwaine insisted, turning briefly before heading back the way he had come.

Ron nodded. 'Okay, eight it is. See you there.'

He headed back towards his van, looking forward to the evening, but he was sure he wouldn't like what Dwaine had to say about the camp. First, he had to find the others, as he didn't have long to convince them.

Convince them?

But what about John? He had his doubts about him, but he had looked after the three of them, and Ron was sure that if they were to leave, they could do with having him around. *Fuck it!* he thought. He would tell him, but he just hoped he could convince him, convince them all.

36

Day 4

PARLIAMENT HILL

8.03 p.m.

John stood with his arms folded, leaning against the kitchen sink, head slightly bowed, hoping none of his colleagues were aware of where he was. He knew he had to go with them and find out what the hell was going on, and Ron had sounded convincing, and had said a soldier would be accompanying them. John was convinced the others had their doubts, and he had had an earbashing from Fiona when he mentioned it to her and Debbie, though Debbie had said they should go along just to hear him out, kind of making the peace. Debbie and Fiona were sat on a makeshift bed, Fiona with her head down, looking as if she wished she was anywhere else but there, while Debbie offered an encouraging smile.

Mary and her husband, along with Mathew, were sat on the tiny settee, Mary's husband talking to his son. He did not want to be there either, but had been dragged along by Mary. Mathew was doing most of the talking, going on about how he had met one of his old school friends, and how they had made loads of new mates and had been playing football for most of the day, talking about setting up five-a-side teams and playing a knockout competition the following day or so.

As for Ron, he remained agitated, constantly glancing at his watch and then out of the van window, hoping and praying the soldier would show, prove he wasn't being paranoid. He had seen the look in John's eyes when he struggled to explain, and recalled him crossing his arms and sighing, but showing a little interest when he told him about the soldier. Mary had been a little easier to convince, but with each minute that passed it seemed to Ron that he was losing their trust, and he knew the policeman's patience would run out if he didn't deliver. Then there was the question of whose side the policeman would take if this were the case. He knew deep down that John still had responsibilities and a duty; it was like a marriage to people like him, the only lasting relationship he would ever have.

Then came the knock Ron had been waiting for and in came a flustered young man, dressed causally. He looked a little startled as he glanced around, not expecting so many people. Then another man entered – tall, a little overweight and ageing. He had a smile on his face that made him look older and he seemed relaxed. He immediately began shaking everyone's hand and introduced himself as Paul, telling them he worked behind the scenes at the camp, although not wanting to go into too much detail.

'I am not sure how much Ron has told you, but basically we have to get out of here,' Dwaine said, getting straight to the point, observing them one by one, expecting some scepticism.

'Could you give us a little more detail on why the urgency to leave?' John asked, intrigued by what the two men had to say. He wanted to hear it from the horse's mouth, though, as the older man did not look like a soldier; perhaps he was an officer.

'Making it as simple as possible, this camp was set up for two reasons: one, as a checkpoint, to find out who's who and so on, and then move most of them on to other camps, and two, as a camp to contain the virus, those possibly at risk of being infected, like yourselves, having to remain here. That is why they will be asking for a blood sample from you again soon. Not only does it house yourselves and other people who may be at risk, but the crazed as well, in those big houses over there. Now, as you're probably aware, the virus only infected a certain number of people; apparently, it only affects a certain blood group, while in the other blood groups it lies dormant, and for the blood group it does affect it becomes an aggressive virus, basically taking away rationality and making them monsters, deadly monsters. This place is a ticking time bomb,' Paul said, constantly glancing at them, talking like a politician.

'Why the hell would they house the crazed? Why not just kill them?' Jamie asked, frowning, shocked by what he was hearing.

'Listen, I shouldn't be saying this, and it mustn't leave this room, but there are suspicions that this whole disease was released by our own government. I don't know the exact details, but they are trying to clean it up, find a cure for those infected and testing people like yourselves with a similar blood group. The reason for the urgency to leave is that I heard they are getting desperate,' Paul said, his eyes darting around.

'Sounds absurd,' Jamie said. 'We are just in a temporary shelter until they can sort things out. That's what we were told on arrival, and it's all over the news.'

'Then answer this, Jamie, why have the news reporters not been allowed within the infected areas? What are they trying to hide from the press? So, we intend to get the hell out of here, and a group of us will be leaving at eleven tonight. There is limited space for yourselves, and it's your choice,' Paul said, and then added, 'I'm just trying to do my bit by saving you people, prove that not all members of authority are heartless bastards.'

Paul patted Dwaine on his shoulder, who just nodded.

'Listen, thanks for putting yourselves out like this and offering to help us get out. Let us think it over, eh?' John said, smiling.

'Be near the canteen for eleven if you wish to go, and this offer is only open to you people, no more,' Dwaine said, continuing to observe the group.

Ron gave a nod, patted the lad on his back and watched them leave.

Then he turned to the others and said, 'I'm going. I don't intend to hang around and become one of those things, or be killed by them if they should escape.'

Mary, Jamie and Mathew got up to leave, Jamie saying they would think it over. Debbie and Fiona followed them.

John remained and glanced at Ron.

'Do you actually believe those two? And what exactly is this Paul's job?'

Ron thought for a moment. For some reason he didn't quite trust them, but he was desperate to get out of the camp and find his daughter, and when you are that desperate, you will take any chance there is.

'Yes, I do think he is telling the truth,' Ron said finally, meeting the policeman's eyes.

37

Day 4

PARLIAMENT HILL

8.37 p.m.

'Surely you don't believe any of that rubbish,' Jamie said as they entered the van, wondering why he had agreed to go through with it.

'Well, Ron and John seemed convinced, and there is something about this camp that's not quite right, you even said so yourself,' Mary said, sitting down, not making eye contact; she recalled the only time they had made brief eye contact recently was when they were reunited.

She remembered them walking away from the cabin, his hand slipping out of hers, not wanting to hold it for too long. She knew then that she was in for a hard time. Then she recalled the moment they got to their van, when Jamie ordered Mathew to go to his room and grabbed Mary by the arm, asking her if she was out of her mind to have risked her life and Mathew's just to try to reach a office block. He told her how some soldier had told him what she had done, and asked her if she realised how embarrassed he felt. She accepted she had done the wrong thing, but not once had he apologised for his outburst; but perhaps she had deserved it.

'There is a sense of anxiety in the air, and those two seem paranoid and troublemakers. Perhaps the only thing wrong with this camp is them,' Jamie said. He sat down next to Mary and said, 'When all this happened, all I wanted to do was head home and be with you, be with the both of you, nothing else mattered, but we were told we had to evacuate immediately. No time to think or act, we just boarded a bus and headed out here, and believe me, it was chaos. Cars, buses, army personnel everywhere, the roads gridlocked. On the first night, some of us had to sleep in tents, and then the following day most of the other vans arrived. It was heartbreaking, and believe me, I so wanted to break away, find you two no matter what and get the hell out of London, but I knew it would be too risky, so I decided to rely on the authorities to find you. And as the days went by, it wasn't too bad, but I made myself a promise that when I saw you again I would not let the two of you go anywhere without me, or take any risks that may put us in danger. I know I had a go at you yesterday, but I was just so angry, and to be honest I have a feeling this whole idea of leaving the compound would be a big mistake…'

He spoke without looking at her. Then he paused as his mobile bleeped. He glanced at the screen and began reading a message, after which he said, while texting away, 'However, if you really want to leave, then so be it, we'll go. But I am not one hundred per cent happy with it, and we are still waiting on news about your cousin.' He smiled at her. 'If you really do want to go once we're out, we could always split from the rest and head for your brother's. You did say he was fine when you spoke to him earlier.'

A hint of a change of heart in his voice, Mary thought, *a possible distraction persuading him, but what could that distraction have been?* Then again, he had been distracted a lot recently, his head always elsewhere. Many a time she had wondered why, but had put it down to his job. Though she had begun to wonder, the rumours and banter of his colleagues returning to haunt her.

'The policeman and Ron are pretty clever and cool to be with,' Mathew said. It all seemed like a dangerous adventure to him, one he had had the pleasure of telling all of his newfound mates about, making him feel like a young Indiana Jones, popular. And he was ready for his next adventure; it was definitely more exciting than a football tournament.

'I say we go along,' he said chirpily.

'These two guys seem to have made an impression on you,' Jamie said, finally making eye contact with Mary and seeming to be fully conscious of her.

His eyes appeared to be probing into her mind, and for the first time in her life she felt almost frightened by it.

38

Day 4

PARLIAMENT HILL

8.23 p.m.

As John headed back to the van he was sharing with Debbie and Fiona, he thought about everything he had just heard, everything he had recorded. It seemed to him that these two men were desperate to leave, but why? And why did they want them to join them? He then recalled talking to a few of his colleagues earlier, wanting to know when he would be back on duty, and he had told them about the bank and the death of Margaret, Lisa and Keith. They had told him they would collect the bodies and that he would be back on duty in a few days; they just needed to take another blood sample to make sure he would not be affected by the virus, as it was airborne. The same chemicals they had used to scramble technology had poisoned certain people, confusing their minds and speeding up their metabolism. Most of those infected would die within a week, and the virus could not be passed on by bites, unless you were receptive to it and of the same blood group as those infected. Also, you would have to come into contact with their blood and it would have to enter your bloodstream, so it was very unlikely. On a good note, they told him they had had a possible breakthrough with how to treat the virus, and would give everyone in the country an inoculation just to be safe. They had let slip that there had been four arrests so far, one a government official. John was sure the government official would try to strike a deal, wanting a lighter sentence for name dropping; they were damn good at looking after themselves. He was sure the two men Ron had introduced them to knew something, and he was intrigued to find out what and to start putting together his evidence. He was sure of one thing – whatever the others decided to do, he owed it to them to look out for them, even if it meant going along with their plan; he believed the dead deserved justice.

He knew he would have to hear Fiona's opinion about it upon returning to the van. She would have made a great detective. He smiled to himself. Perhaps he could talk her into coming along, but could he separate her and Debbie? No, he couldn't risk Debbie's safety. There was only one thing to do, and that was to have a cigarette, make Fiona wait with her opinion. He smiled again, as he knew how she hated him smoking, the smell of tobacco, but he needed it to chill out before facing her.

'So, you took us to that pokey van for that?' Fiona said as he entered.

She was leaning against the sink with her arms folded.

He forced a smile and then sat down next to Debbie, kissing her on the cheek, knowing Fiona would be wilder because he had made her wait.

'What do you think?' Debbie asked.

But before he could reply, Fiona tutted and said, 'What I saw and heard, I thought it was a joke. Seems like you've been going around with a bunch of goofs, something like a Harry Potter convention. I wouldn't trust any of them, no, no way would I go along with those crazy plans. And if you do decide to, make sure that when you get caught you don't tell the authorities we had anything to do with it. We are not losing this luxury home for the likes of you and your rebellion.'

John so wanted to tell her what he thought of her, to hurt her verbally and physically. She was the thorn in his side, the reason he was sure Debbie had never truly committed to him, the bloody distraction that always had a way of coming between them, filling Debbie with her ideas. A manipulative bitch, a witch, that's what John saw when he looked at her.

'They may be a bunch of goofs, but we survived some harsh conditions,' John said, trying to keep his voice even, trying not to let his feelings or thoughts spill out, even though they were aching to.

'Well, we have all been through harsh conditions,' Fiona snapped back.

'Fiona, I have heard your story and so has the rest of the camp, but you made your amazing escape before it became serious. You have refused to listen to my story, but now you are going to hear it. I was on the front line, and I know what those things are capable of. I even had the dissatisfaction of watching them tear two people to pieces whom I was trying to save. And yes, I have also had the dissatisfaction of shooting some of them dead,' John said, wanting to say so much more, but he knew he was wasting his time.

Fiona stood in front of John and Debbie, head bowed and arms still folded, trying to look interested in what John was saying.

'And the point you are trying to make is...? Do you want an OBE or some other medal? Because as far as I'm concerned, that is all you have ever been interested in, self-glory. And anyway, I am sure there are people who have been through a hell of a lot worse than you.'

'I am not denying that, and all I am concerned about is our welfare, not self-glory. The reason I have said what I have and shown my concern regarding what's happening is because I don't want those crazed who they have caged up breaking out and attacking us. I would sooner be a million miles from here in case that happens, and it's not a chance I want to take. Like I said, they are serious predators, ruthless.'

John allowed himself to smile, as he could see Fiona looking deflated by what he had said. It seemed he had actually stunned her into thinking, made her realise she may die if those things escaped. Even though John was sure there weren't any crazed in there, he thought it would be nice to frighten her, and he was hoping Debbie would see how selfish she was when it came to worrying about others. Perhaps he had said enough to entice Fiona to go with them.

Fiona had her mobile in her hand and started texting away. Without looking at either of them, she said, 'Let's all think it over, eh?'

John smiled, feeling proud of himself, and before she could consider any form of retaliation he kissed Debbie on the cheek, got to his feet and left the van. As he was closing the door, he could hear Fiona expressing her concerns to Debbie regarding what he had said about the crazed, and he was sure she would be suggesting they leave upon his return. But for now he had two things to do, the first being to enjoy a cigarette.

His moment of victory.

39

Day 4

PARLIAMENT HILL

10.17 p.m.

'Come quickly!' Fiona said, bursting into John's dream.

Before he could get his bearings or ask any questions, Fiona had left, leaving the bedroom door wide open, frost and the sound of gunfire filling the room.

At first John glanced around, wondering what was happening. He didn't realise he had fallen asleep and had only gone for a lie down to give Fiona and Debbie a little time to themselves, as they were still unsure what they wanted to do. They had been debating in the other room and he had tried his best to put Debbie off the idea, as he didn't want to risk her life. He had even arranged for a colleague to look out for her while he was gone. While he was alone in the bedroom, before he had fallen asleep, he had been thinking things through. One of his colleagues had come up with a plan which should guarantee both of them a promotion at the very least. And his colleague had done a little searching for him, looking into Ron's daughter's whereabouts. He had heard rumours of where she might be, but Brighton hadn't been mentioned.

He stepped out of the room to see the caravan door open and both Fiona and Debbie outside, staring and pointing into the distance. He yawned, rubbed the ache of sleep from his eyes and stepped out of the van.

'What the hell...?' he said, and then paused.

There were flames billowing from the direction of the large warehouse buildings the soldier had told them about, though it was difficult to see what was happening, as the group of trees hid most of the area. A jeering crowd could be heard and the alarming sound of gunfire, but who was firing the guns?

'What the hell is going on?' he said, thinking people were probably pissed off having not been told anything and having seen so much on the Internet, fuelling their anger.

'There are rumours circulating that there are some of the crazed in those large buildings down there, and people are pissed off and want to burn them all to death,' said a man standing not far from John.

The man snuggled into his jacket, trying to keep warm. Lights had been switched on all around as people stared from caravans.

'If they are in there, they are bound to escape now,' came another voice; a woman, with a child by her side.

John glanced around, noticing more people had appeared. Then some began arguing as people took sides, some defending the authorities, others challenging them. He wanted to reassure them that everything was going to be alright, but wasn't sure what was going to happen either. Suddenly, a man came running towards them, shouting that all hell had broken loose down there. He ran straight past them all and continued to shout. People started to emerge from the vans, demanding to know what was happening, and then the muttering started, then the panic, people grabbing their loved ones and running. But where were they running to?

'I think we should take up your friend's offer and get the hell out of here,' Fiona said, appearing at his side.

'I suppose you'll be joining us now,' came a voice from behind them.

All three turned to see Ron sitting in a jeep, with Mary, Jamie and Mathew, another jeep in tow with vacant seats.

'Well, what are you waiting for?' Ron said, offering them all a smile.

All three of them scrambled on-board, and as they did so, other people raced over, holding children up and screaming how they needed to save their child. But Dwaine fired warning shots into the air and people ducked; then both jeeps sped away, leaving the fading noise of protest and screaming behind.

They whipped through the camp, swerving between the vans and dodging people who desperately tried to flag them down, everybody wanting out of that crazy camp.

As they approached the main exit, a guard raised his rifle at them, shouting something in their direction.

Ron ducked and ordered the others to follow suit, and as Mary, Jamie and Mathew did so, they heard gunshots and felt the jeep shudder as it smashed through the metal sheet gates and the barricades. Gunshots continued to ring out, but faded as they hit the open road.

Ron sat up and glanced at Dwaine, who was smiling.

'We are home and dry, brother.'

Ron cheered, Mary and Jamie smiled at each other, but Dwaine and the driver just shared a look, a look that Ron was sure was relief.

John studied the two men in the front seats. Paul was in the passenger seat, while the skinny young man was driving, his face pale and clammy, hands gripping firmly onto the steering wheel. Paul looked very relaxed and unfazed by the madness that had unfolded, almost relieved. The young man was dressed in army clothing, and John guessed he was about nineteen, probably a newish recruit.

'You're not on duty now, PC, just relax,' Fiona said, smiling and nudging John.

Fiona was just glad to be out of that place, which had become a hellhole. At least they were alive, and with regards to the others, as far as she was concerned they could all go to hell, Justin included.

They sat in silence for over an hour, John noticing the signs indicated they were travelling south. Initially they kept to the minor roads as much as possible, headlights switched off. Whilst the drivers wore night goggles, the others just stared blindly into the darkness; London was silent. They were all thinking about what they had seen and heard, touched and hurt by the misery and hysteria. For the second part of the journey they used the main roads, and noticed the lamps were lit, the electric signs were working and there were other drivers; they were back in civilisation.

'So, where are we destined for?' Fiona asked the driver, wondering if the young man had a voice.

Paul offered her a smile, but no reply.

She glanced at John and Debbie, shrugged and rolled her eyes.

Then five minutes later, they turned off the main road and headed down a country lane, moments later turning onto a farm, the gravel crunching under the tyres, before finally coming to a halt outside the farmhouse.

Paul jumped out of the jeep, and when his guests had done the same, he said, 'I think it would be best if we stay here for the night, then push on in the morning.'

John, Ron and the others glanced at each other and shrugged their approval. John accepted a cigarette from Ron and watched the four men that had rescued them. They were whispering, Paul dishing out orders and then heading into the farmhouse with the driver of the jeep Ron had travelled in. Ron glanced around the farm as his eyes began to adapt to the darkness, and saw that there was a barn nearby. The farm itself was surrounded by trees, almost hiding the place, and making it seem even darker, despite the moonlight.

Dwaine approached them and requested they join them in the house. They all followed without question, though John remained at the rear.

They entered the kitchen, noticing it was littered with the remnants of breakfast, flies feeding on the leftovers, and a stench in the air of gone-off milk.

'So, do you know the owners of this place?' John asked, wondering why this particular farm.

Dwaine stared at John, and John realised the young man was suspicious of him.

'You're a policeman, right?' Dwaine said.

John nodded and then said, 'The farm?' not wanting the young man to change the subject.

'It belongs to me,' Paul said, stepping in to the kitchen. He glanced at Dwaine and said, 'How about showing the guests to their rooms? Though I'm sure Ron and John will stay with me for a short chat. And please, everybody, no mobile phone use, we can't afford to be traced or call people just yet. They will want us back if they can get their hands on us.' Paul offered Mary a smile and added, 'I'm so sorry if that is inconvenient.'

Paul, John and Ron watched them all leave the kitchen, Paul offering them another smile, something he seemed to give generously.

He turned to John and Ron and said, 'So come on, tell me, why were you in the city for such a long time before joining the rescue centre?'

John glanced at Ron, who was frowning, so John thought about what he wanted to say, delayed for a while and then said, 'We had a little business to attend to.'

He did not look at Ron and just focused on Paul, who stared back at him looking thoughtful. Dwaine reappeared and explained that the others were waiting for them.

'It's been a long day, and we intend to be on the move by late morning tomorrow,' Paul said, probing them with his eyes.

'Where are we going?' John said.

Dwaine glanced at Ron and said, 'Ron said something about it being pretty safe in Brighton.'

Ron gave a slight nod, thinking about his daughter. He had texted her less than an hour ago to let her know he was on his way and was waiting for her reply; he was waiting for many replies, and it was out of character for her to not do so, which frustrated him.

'Unless you have somewhere else we need to head to first...' Paul said to John.

John didn't reply and headed for the stairs, knowing secrets would play to their advantage.

There were four rooms on the second floor: two large bedrooms, a small bedroom and a bathroom. The bedrooms were simply furnished, with beds, a bedside cabinet and a wardrobe; none had a television. Ron took the smallest, while Mary's family were in one of the larger bedrooms. John insisted his party take the front bedroom, overlooking the yard.

Ron followed Debbie, Fiona and John into their room, wanting to share their company before going alone, something he would have to get used to again, though it was a harrowing thought. While he made small talk with Debbie and Fiona, talking about family and friends, John stared out of the window, noticing how the two drivers had moved the vehicles into a barn, out of sight. He was intrigued to know what else was in there.

He made his excuses to leave the room, stating he needed to use the bathroom, but instead he headed in the direction of the landing, determined to try to overhear something, to find out a little more about these people; then he would know how to execute his plan.

John could hear them, but it was not loud enough for him to make out what they were saying, so he crept down the stairs, trying not to make a sound, as he had noticed going up the stairs that the boards had a habit of creaking. He paused when he got to the bottom step and listened carefully.

'Listen, you're all going to be looked after. They should get here about eleven.' The voice was Paul's. He mumbled something, and they all laughed.

'But what are we going to do with them?' Dwaine asked.

'We need to know what they have been hiding or shifting in London so we can salvage something; I promised you that,' Paul said.

Dwaine's reply was fast, and all John could make out was the word rid, which was said more than once.

John smiled, his suspicions confirmed. He had been so sure that Paul believed they had something to hide and was hoping they would lead them there; all four of them were probably soldiers of fortune. But then, perhaps there was more to them than that. John was sure that when they found nothing, and learned that he had been snooping around, they would kill them. He had to execute his plan, now.

'What on earth is the matter with you?' Ron said as John stepped back into the room.

John was thinking of the best way forward for them all, but knew they deserved an explanation.

'Well?' Fiona said, arms folded, getting annoyed with him.

'Just wait here,' John said, wanting to tell Jamie and Mary at the same time as the others.

They all stood around waiting for an explanation, apart from Mathew, who was sound asleep.

John told them what he had overheard, hoping it was enough to make them realise they were all in trouble unless they acted. Deep down he hadn't wanted it to come to this, not with Debbie and Mary's family involved, so now his priority was to save them.

'If it is true what you are saying, we obviously have to get the hell out of here,' Fiona said, heading in the direction of the door.

'Wait a minute, we can't just go marching through the door. I mean, it could just be idle chat, you know, lads down there having a few beers, and they were glad to get out as it was hell there; you know, just pissed kids talking stupid,' Ron said, convinced John was overreacting.

'I'm not sure,' Jamie said, not trusting the four men downstairs.

'Listen, these guys aren't good news and they will do us harm. We seriously have to get out of here,' John said, texting away on his mobile and putting his plan into action. He had planned to call his colleague, but recalled the tracker he was wearing and remembered agreeing he would just send a text when they were ready; he didn't want to panic the others.

They were all torn as to what was the right thing to do, all confused and not sure what to do or think.

John watched and waited, feeling frustrated by their doubt, knowing they would need convincing, but how could he do that when they needed to act straightaway?

40

Day 5

SUSSEX

12.07 a.m.

'I just don't know what to say,' Ron explained, trying to understand what John had said, sure that he was wrong.

'I know you all have your doubts, but all I can say is, why don't some of you come downstairs and listen?' John said, feeling a little annoyed.

Then he recalled it had been this way for most of his life, being a policeman, people always doubting him, the general public not giving him enough credit, when there he was trying to save them.

'So let's say you're right, what do we do?' Jamie asked.

'Basically we have to creep out of here, get those vehicles and then get well away from this farm,' John said, knowing it would definitely be easier said than done. There was more to his plan than that, but it was on a need-to-know basis.

'Well, it's no good us all charging down there, so who will go and listen?' Ron said, not liking it, but wanting to prove the policeman wrong, still feeling a little stung from his sneakiness and when he had laughed at him earlier.

What was really annoying Ron was how the policeman was doing an awful lot of texting, more than likely keeping in touch with his police buddies back at Parliament Hill. Ron was sure he was after a promotion, probably to impress Debbie, make up for not being there for her.

'How about us four?' Fiona said, glancing at Ron, John and Jamie.

They all agreed.

'But before we go, just remember, if you are overreacting they will be extremely pissed off when they find out,' Ron said.

And when no reply came, he just followed, angry that John had made the assumptions he had, and when he was proven wrong, he wanted him to apologise to them all, including the four men that had saved them; yes, that would teach him.

When they had made it to the bottom of the stairs, they could hear laughter, a little banter, but nothing unusual.

'I think we are wasting…' Ron said.

He paused when they heard Paul say, 'I imagine they could have hidden large quantities of money; I mean, come on, think about it, a tube worker obviously knows his way around, and a policeman, the others a decoy. You boys are going to be so rich.'

'Now do you believe me about getting out of here?' John whispered.

Nobody argued.

Ron took his mobile out of his pocket selected a phone number, the one Libby had recently used to text him on, and pressed call. A mobile in the other room started ringing. He ended the call and bowed his head to hide the pain he was feeling. No Libby waiting at Brighton, then.

Fiona and Jamie stared at Ron, wondering why he had called one of the men's mobiles. But John knew why, and wished he had said something earlier, but he promised himself he would tell Ron at some point.

'Go upstairs and get the others ready while we sort out the vehicles,' John said to Jamie, knowing there would be no arguments from anyone now. They had to act quickly, just in case.

Jamie nodded, accepting what he had to do, and then smiled faintly at Fiona, who smiled back.

John, Ron and Fiona stepped out into the blackened night; it was silent apart from the rustling of the chill wind through the trees and bushes.

'Listen, as soon as we get to the jeeps, I'll go for the others. Then I want you all to get the hell out of here,' John said as they got further away from the house and nearer to the barn.

'I take it you are not joining us, then?' Ron said, wondering again what the policeman was up to, but he knew he wouldn't tell him and believed he was definitely after all the glory.

'Please, just do as I say,' John said. He couldn't tell them anything, just in case something went wrong, as he didn't know how they might react under interrogation.

'Perhaps it would have been a good idea to bring a torch with us,' Fiona said, almost tripping over something in the dark.

'No torch, no give away; we work like a blind man, and use our other senses to their max,' John said.

Nobody argued and just followed, slowing on their approach to the barn. Once in inside, they remained stationary for a minute or two until their eyes adjusted to the darkness, just enough so they could see the outline of the vehicles.

'So, you know how to hot-wire these things?' Fiona asked John.

He shrugged, climbed into one and then began removing the dashboard, a little penlight he had taken out of his pocket being the only source of light.

'I will get it ready, as I don't want to hot-wire it until you're all ready to leave,' he said, concentrating on the wires he was now examining. 'Should be pretty easy, as it's an old vehicle,' he said a moment later.

Ron stood near the entrance on guard, wishing the two of them would be a little quieter. Suddenly, he could see light coming from the house as the door opened.

'Oh shit,' he said. Turning to the others, he said, 'Somebody's coming from the house.'

John climbed from the vehicle and headed over to Ron, Fiona close behind.

It was the two young soldiers, both carrying guns and torches; perhaps they were doing a patrol, or maybe Paul had got wise to what was going on. John was sure they were a little nervous and would pull the trigger at the slightest movement.

'What the fuck are we going to do now?' Fiona asked.

There was no reply as Ron and John tried to think of a plan.

They all glanced behind them into the blackened barn and said in unison, 'We have to hide.'

All three stumbled to the rear of the vehicles and crouched down, trying to calm their breathing and stay still, a thousand thoughts going through their minds of what may happen to them. Then they all froze as a torch was shone into the barn, one of the men stating how he hadn't left the door open, and then the sound of guns clicking followed by the two men mumbling.

'We know someone is in here. Just stand up and show yourself, then nobody gets hurt.' The voice sounded nervous.

Before John and Ron could consider what to do, Fiona had stood up, her hands in the air, begging them to not shoot. John and Ron shared a look of disbelief before also standing with their arms raised.

Paul had a grin on his face as they were led back to the farmhouse.

'So, you were going to steal the jeeps, then what? Head into London for your ill gains?'

'That's right,' Fiona said, smirking, not sure what he were talking about. But she knew that while you had something that somebody else wanted, they wouldn't kill you. She just hoped John had a backup plan.

The young soldiers led the three of them into the living quarters, where Mary, Jamie, Debbie and Mathew were sitting on the sofas. There was a large flat-screen television on the wall, and it was on the news channel.

'There are reports of a disturbance at Parliament Hill, during which two jeeps were stolen. One of the men now wanted in connection with the biological warfare attack on London has recently been named as a suspect after arrests were made. And within the next few hours it is believed that there will be a statement from the government and the Mayor of London...'

Paul turned off the television.

'Now, I want you all to sit in here and behave yourselves, and I require your mobiles,' he said, holding his hand out to John, Ron and Fiona.

'You're one of those they're after, aren't you?' Ron said, pissed off about how he had been used, about how cruel they had been to him.

Paul just smiled and ordered the two young men and Dwaine out of the room so that he could speak to them alone. He watched them leave, closed the door and then turned to face his guests.

'There are no hidden belongings in London, are there?' Paul said to John. 'You lied to those boys out there, and believe me, they are going to be so pissed when they find out. Then again, why should I care? All I want is to get out of the country, as I have been promised.'

Paul paused and smiled, wondering whether to tell them, but he would never see them again, and sooner or later they would hear about it anyway; not his version though, not the undiluted truth.

'I worked in Bio Warfare for the government as one of the head scientists. We were creating a bomb that could neutralise all forms of communication, scrambling them for many days, which would advance warfare. Me and a few colleagues had heard that the government was planning to shelve our creation, make us all redundant, throw us out with the rubbish as if we were worthless; it was a bloody insult. So that's when we schemed with our colleagues to sell our creation to other countries, possibly raise enough money to become an independent lab. We had a party very interested, but they wanted to see what it was capable of.'

He smiled when he saw how shocked they all were.

'Don't worry, the government had heard that something was going to happen, which is why they were constructing that place at Parliament Hill and elsewhere, but they didn't know who was involved. We were all integrated, but none of us cracked. Then when it did happen, we didn't expect it to affect people the way it did. I fled to the rescue centre and helped out there as much as I could, hoping they wouldn't suspect me, as there were at least sixty in our department and any of them could have carried out the threat. Then, when the government official was arrested, I knew it was only a matter of time until I was named. So I poisoned the mind of those young boys out there with theories and false promises, and you all fitted into my plan perfectly.'

Paul smiled again, enjoying his moment of genius. The horror was evident on all of their faces, but why should he care? He only needed them for a little while longer, until the following day.

41

Day 5

SUSSEX

10.23 a.m.

They had stayed in the one room all night, Mathew having slept on Mary's lap for most of it while she stroked his hair. Not once had she spoken to Jamie; in fact, they had hardly even looked at each other. During the night it seemed as if Mary had gained an insight into their relationship, feeling certain whom Jamie really wanted to be with. In the back of her mind she had known it would come to this, and had believed back when they first met that Jamie only ever wanted her for one thing. Over the years, as his ability to get what he wanted became less likely, the more he looked elsewhere and the harder she had tried to make it work. Bastard, that was what he was in her eyes. Then again, perhaps it was time for them both to move on; that is if they were able to get out of the situation alive. She believed that she and Mathew should go to her parents, who cared about them and had been so upset and relieved when she called them. As for her cousin Kelly, she had a bad feeling about her welfare. She knew she had a temper and would have more than likely fought with those crazed things, and died fighting.

Ron had not slept either, with no sleeping pills or whisky to help him, so he had spent most of the night staring at them all. He sensed Mary and Jamie had had a disagreement, and imagined they had been struggling as a family for quite a while. He also found himself staring at Fiona, realising he had seen her before, in the picture he had in his pocket. Fiona and Jamie were certainly showing an awful lot of interest in each other, and right in front of Mary, which made Ron want to punch the man's head in, something he believed he deserved. He had then spent most of the night going out of his mind with worry about his Libby, but trying to believe they would all get out of there alive and he would somehow see his daughter again. He had to think positively.

As for John, he had also remained awake, glancing at Ron from time to time, considering telling him about his Libby. But he chose not to, not yet, as he didn't want it to lead to erratic behaviour, didn't want to unbalance anything. He would sooner let the authorities tell him the news when it was all over; that she had been arrested for looting, apparently had taken a beating, the army personnel being a little heavy-handed with her, and was now in a coma. John had also looked at Debbie, who had been talking to Ron, Mary and of course Fiona and Jamie. She had spent quite some time in their company, which frustrated him, and when dawn arrived he had found himself hating Fiona more than ever.

Suddenly, the door opened and in stepped Paul, a smile on his face.

'Good morning, all! I do hope you have all slept well and yes, we are on the move, right now in fact. So chop-chop!'

'And what on earth do you intend to do with us?' Jamie asked, standing next to Fiona, Mary and Mathew.

'We are going for a drive, but don't worry, you won't be hurt,' Paul said, a gun in his hand; a hand pistol, with a silencer.

He was joined by Dwaine, and the two young lads.

Paul glanced at Mathew and said, 'Look away, son.'

Sensing danger, Mary pulled him close to her.

Paul calmly turned to his three young friends and pointed the gun at them.

'Fuck…' one of the young men managed before his head exploded.

'No…' said the second as a bullet tore through his brain.

'No, man, no, please,' Dwaine said as a bullet burst into his forehead, throwing him on top of the lifeless bodies of the other two men.

'What the fuck!' Ron said, staring at the three bodies fitting on the floor.

Paul shrugged his shoulders and smiled.

'We don't need them any more. Trust me, you are all going to be safe now. I will drop you off somewhere, but then I have to go.'

A tall man, with a weathered face and grey hair, strode over to the bodies, a small, slim woman in tow.

'Are we ready to get the hell out of here?' the tall man said.

Paul gave a quick nod and then said, 'Go to the van and get it ready. I'll bring the others out in a moment.'

Paul's two accomplices stared for a moment at the hostages, and then without another word smiled and left.

'Now, behave yourselves, and I give you my word, nobody gets hurt,' Paul said.

He glanced out of the window, and then turned to them and asked them to leave, to head for the van out in the yard. They did as he said, having to stride over the three lukewarm bodies that were still grunting and groaning, with the occasional twitching of nerves.

The van doors were open, but Paul's two accomplices were nowhere to be seen, and his hostages just stood in front of him, wondering what to do.

'What the fuck?' Paul said, sensing the danger, feeling that something wasn't quite right.

'DROP THE GUN, DROP THE GUN. WE HAVE YOU SURROUNDED, SO DROP THE GUN.'

Paul pointed the gun at Mathew, who was standing two yards in front of him, and shouted, 'THE BOY GETS IT UNLESS YOU LET ME GO.'

'MUM, MUM,' Mathew shrieked, starting to cry.

'NOT MATHEW, PLEASE NOT MY BOY, HE'S ALL I HAVE,' Mary screamed, holding him tight.

'I MEAN IT, THE BOY DIES,' Paul shouted, glancing around, wondering where the armed police were. He knew he only had seconds before they shot him, unless he acted, did something alarming to prove he was for real.

Suddenly, Ron rushed in front of Mathew and Mary, shielding them from what may happen, wanting to fulfil his promise that they would not be harmed. Jamie pulled Fiona close, Debbie by their side. John noticed how dazed Paul looked; he had taken his eye off them for that split second, long enough for him to act, and he so wanted this man to be brought to justice, to face the courts for what he had done. Keith, Margaret, Lisa and the many, many more deserved that.

He lunged forward and struck Paul across the face with his elbow, and Paul stumbled backwards. They grappled with each other, and John grabbed the hand in which Paul held the gun, wanting to take it from him, but Paul pulled the trigger and two or three shots were fired. But John refused to let go, and in his blind fury he managed to hit him a few times, sending Paul crashing to the ground.

'SHE'S BEEN HIT, SHE'S BEEN FUCKING HIT!' Fiona shrieked.

John jumped on top of Paul and began hitting him with his fists, reliving the horror he had witnessed, every punch packing the power of every terrifying moment, blood splattering everywhere, the sound of bones crunching. Paul's face was now a mass of blood, and John felt his knuckles burning, his hand cramping, but he continued to hit him.

Suddenly, he was dragged away by two officers, one shouting his name, ordering him to stop.

And for a short while John lay on his back, regaining his breath, and when the mist cleared and his breathing slowed, he got to his feet and noticed there was an ambulance team trying to resuscitate Paul. He then turned to see Fiona kneeling on the floor, cradling Debbie in her arms.

'YOU BASTARD, YOU BASTARD! YOU KILLED HER, YOU FUCKING KILLED HER!' Fiona shouted at him.

John rushed over to see Debbie's head slumped to one side, her eyes wide and a bullet hole in her temple; one of the three bullets. He turned away, shaking, and then let out a mighty cry.

'AWWWWWWWWWWWWWW! WHY FUCKING WHY?'

He slumped to the ground and noticed the gun at his feet, the one that had fired the fatal shot. He picked it up. He thought of the policeman he had taken the gun from, about Keith he had given the gun to, and suddenly the urge came; he was so angry, so upset. He pointed the gun at his own head.

'JOHN, NO! PUT THE GUN DOWN.'

He pulled the trigger.